Arnold E. Sadi

The Gulistan

Being the Rose Garden of Sadi, the First Four Babs

Arnold E. Sadi

The Gulistan
Being the Rose Garden of Sadi, the First Four Babs

ISBN/EAN: 9783337100490

Printed in Europe, USA, Canada, Australia, Japan

Cover: Foto ©Andreas Hilbeck / pixelio.de

More available books at **www.hansebooks.com**

FROM THE PERSIAN

THE GULISTAN

BEING THE

ROSE-GARDEN OF SHAIKH SA'DI

The first four Babs, or "Gateways"

TRANSLATED IN PROSE AND VERSE BY

SIR EDWIN ARNOLD

K.C.I.E., C.S.I.

Author of "The Light of Asia" etc.

HARPER & BROTHERS PUBLISHERS

NEW YORK AND LONDON

1899

CONTENTS

AUTHOR'S PREFACE

Extract from article in LITERATURE, November 12, 1898

SA'DI

OF late, when I have wished—in my study and among my books—to take refuge from politics and bodily pain, and that ocean of careless and worthless written work upon which float the scattered islands that are fair and good in current literature, I have betaken myself to good old Sa'di, and especially to his *Gulistan*. The Shaikh was really the Horace and Marco Polo of the Far East combined into one rich and gracious nature. Ancient enough to carry with him a fine flavor of the Old World, he is

as modern and as much for all times as
the Roman poet himself or American
Emerson.

A brilliant romance might be made
out of his life! Born at Shirâz in A.D.
1193, and educated at the famous college
of Baghdad, he set himself in his manhood, with a keen and genial curiosity,
to see and understand the world. Pious,
albeit shrewd and philosophical, he made
at one date or another no less than four-
teen pilgrimages to Mecca; came to
Europe; and wandered through Asia
Minor, Barbary, Abyssinia, Egypt, Syria,
Palestine, Armenia, Arabia, all Persia,
of course, and India. Naturally, in such
wide peregrinations, he met with many
adventures. What a picture might be
painted, for example, of that particular
one when, roaming about the western
coast of Gujerat, he came to the Holy
Shrine of Siva in Pattan-Sumanât, and
nearly paid with his life for his restless
inquisitiveness! Every morning at sun-
rise the image of the god in the great
temple, with its eyes made of dia-

monds and its robes of jewelled gold,
lifted its hands in blessing to all the vo-
taries who flocked from far and near
to witness the mighty miracle. Sa'di,
though a believer in divine things, was
a bit of a sceptic about Darweeshes and
priestly humbug generally, and so, having hidden himself one day behind the
image, he saw the attendant priest work-
ing its arms with a rope, and thereby
"pulling-off" the portent. Unluckily,
the priest also observed Sa'di, and having attempted to capture him, that gen-
tle-hearted but intrepid traveller found
no alternative except to throw the Brah-
man into the deep well of the temple
and to fly for safety, having first, however, smashed the deceitful effigy.

At Delhi he picked up Hindustani as
perfectly as he had acquired Arabic in
Baghdad. He made journeys to Yemen
and even to Ethiopia, and for some time
lived as a renowned and inspired teacher in Damascus. At Baalbec—where
those glorious Corinthian columns still
rise in the green Lebanon valley, majes-

tic relics of the *Trilithon*, or " Temple of the three great stones "—he delivered many spiritual addresses, some of which are still preserved in the second *Risàlah;* and the cultured grace and devout elevation of them even an archbishop might envy. Weary of his Oriental pulpits he dwelt alone for some time in the desert near Jerusalem, till he was made prisoner there or thereabouts by some crusading soldiers, one of whom (it shames our common Christianity to state) is said to have driven his stupid spear - blade through the shoulder of this delicious poet and moralist. Romantically rescued by a wealthy lord of Aleppo, who ransomed him and also gave him a daughter for a wife, Sa'di went off wandering again; nor was it until his seventieth year that he came back to Shirâz, to sit down tranquilly under the protecting shadow of the Sultan Abubakr, and to write, in a little charming garden outside the city, the sweet prose and mystical Sufic poetry of his *Bustan* and *Gulistan.* Truly that "grand old man "

of Persia must have come home full of
garnered wisdom and abounding obser-
vation of men and things, to his lovely
retreat beneath the cypresses and rose-
bushes, where he wrote the " Rose-Garden" and the "Garden of Fragrance."
I have myself elsewhere paraphrased
what the wise old traveller says so elo-
quently of himself, after his many voy-
ages and travels. *Ba dil goftam az Mizr*,
it begins :

*In many lands I have wandered, and
wondered, and listened, and seen ;
And many my friends and companions,
and teachers and lovers have been.*

*And nowhere a corner was there but I
gathered up pleasure and gain ;
From a hundred gardens the rose-blooms,
from a thousand granaries grain ;*

*And I said to my soul in secret, " Oh,
thou who from journeys art come !
It is meet we should bear some token of
love to the stayers at home ;*

AUTHOR'S PREFACE

For where is the traveller brings not from
Nile the sweet green reed,
Or Kashmiri silk, or musk-bags, or coral,
or cardamum seed?"

I was loath from all that Pleasaunce of
the Sun, and his words and ways,
To come to my country giftless, and show-
ing no fruit of my days:

But, if my hands were empty of honey,
and pearls and gold,
There were treasures far sweeter than
honey, and marvellous things to be
told,

Whiter than pearls and brighter than
the cups at a Sultan's feast,
And these I have brought for love-tokens,
from the Lords of Truth, in my East.

Sa'di died at Shiráz, in A.D. 1292,
and notwithstanding his long journeys
and various adventures—in days, moreover, when travel was rugged work,
and Messrs. Cook & Son and Pullman-

cars did not exist—the legend is that he
had reached the wonderful age of 108
years. What a body! and what a mind!
so to have enjoyed Allah's glorious
world with all the beautiful and wise
people, as well as evil and foolish, which
it always contains; and afterwards to
have bequeathed to that world — as a
deathless joy of scholars — a precious
treasure of letters, the exquisite books
mentioned, together with the *Diwân* and
the *Kulliyätt*, and all the rest. As for
Sa'di's *Gulistan* it is a sort of intellectual
pillaw: a literary curry; a kabab of
versatile genius, where grave and gay,
humor and wisdom, laughter and tears
are threaded together on the skewer of
wit, and spiced by a soft worldliness
and gentle stoicism that makes the dish
irresistible, however jaded may be the
mental appetite.

One feels that any one and every one
of taste and breeding must have loved
the Shaikh Maslah-uddin Sa'di al Shirazi
wherever and whenever they met him.
He wins his way into all quiet and wise

hearts, like Horace himself, or Charles
Lamb and Emerson. In the elegant sim-
plicity of his Persian prose and in the
sweetness and subtlety of his verse he remains inimitably and eternally a classic,
and modern writers might go to worse
schools for style and form than to the
grave playfulness of his measured pages,
and to the natural music with which his
paragraphs blend into his poetic *kita'*
and *baita*, like the breeze in the rose-
bushes with the murmurs of the garden-
stream. Sometimes *un peu malin*, he
could indite a work like the *Al Khabi-
sat*, whose pages could not be safely
recommended to the "young person";
but for the major part he is as clean
and wholesome as he is vivacious. His
books are full of graceful and sagacious
sayings. Ouseley calls him "the bright-
est ornament of Persia, the matchless
possessor of piety, genius, and learning."
Vambéry declares: "This great poet
and scholar is an object of veneration
not only to the people of Persia, but to
every Mohammedan in the Asiatic world.

His *Gulistan* is still read with admiration and rapture in the middle of China, as well as on the extremest borders of Africa. European scholars have long since appreciated and admired the undying freshness of his style, his brilliant language, and his witty and telling similitudes." And Jami calls him "the nightingale of the groves of Shiraz."

"They asked me," he writes in the *Gulistan*, "Of whom didst thou learn manners?" I replied: "From the unmannerly. Whatever I saw them do which I disapproved of, that I abstained from doing."

These also are anecdotes of the noble old Shaikh:

"I never complained," he once said, "of my condition but on a single occasion, when my feet were bare, and I had not money to buy shoes; but I saw a man without feet, and became instantly contented with my lot."

Being asked from whom he learned his philosophy, Sa'di replied: "From the blind, because they never advance a step until they have tried the ground."

No one will be without a friend and instructor who can turn from the turmoil of vulgar life to sip the cup of patience and wisdom on the carpet of tranquillity with Shaikh Maslah-uddin Sa'di al Shirazi.

EDWIN ARNOLD.

PREFACE BY SA'DI

By Allah's help now is concluded
this my book, entitled, *The Garden of
Roses*. From beginning to end I have
shunned that evil habit of authors who
collect from by-gone scriptures the
things they write:

*Better wear rags that are entirely thine
Than basely in a borrowed garb to shine.*

These words of Sa'di shall be found,
in the larger part, mirthful and mixed
with pleasantry, for which reason certain of the more purblind folk shoot out
a tongue of reproach, saying that to
tickle the marrow of the brain foolishly,
and to swallow smoke of the lamp un-
profitably, is not the part of the wise.
Yet will men of light and learning, from

whom the true countenance of a discourse is not concealed, be well aware that herein the pearls of good counsel which heal are threaded on strings of right sense ; that the bitter physic of admonition is constantly mingled with the honey of good humor, so that the spirits of listeners grow not sad, and that they remain not exempt from blessings of acceptance.

After my means have I writ this, spending many days thereon. If it entereth not into an ear of welcome, upon the messenger the message rested to deliver it, *Wa bas !*

Oh thou that readest this book, implore for its author the mercy of God, and pardon for him that did transcribe it. It is finished through the might and succor of that King of all Kings who alone bestoweth what is good.

THE GULISTAN

OR

ROSE-GARDEN

OF

SHAIKH SA'DI

Gateway the First

THE MANNER OF KINGS

THE MANNERS OF KINGS

I

I HEARD of a certain King, who had given orders to put to death one of his captives. The helpless wretch, in that hour of despair, set himself to curse his Majesty, in the tongue of his own country, as it hath been said:

Whoever hath washed his hands of living
Utters his mind without misgiving.

And

In straits which no escape afford
The hand takes hold of the edge of the
*   sword.*

The King inquired, "What sayeth he?"

A minister of kindly nature replied :
" He sayeth, in his vernacular, oh, my
lord :

*God's mercy on the merciful
Lighteth; He loves the pitiful."*

On this the desire to take away the
man's life passed from the King's mind.
But another, Wuzeer, who was of different mood, observed : " It becometh not
people of our quality, in presence of
sovereigns, to utter aught save truth.
This fellow did abuse the King, and say
shameful words." The King's face at
such a speech puckered into frowns, and
he said : " Better came that lie from him
than thy truthfulness from thee, since
the lie was of good intent, but the truthfulness builded on malignity." The
Hakims have declared :

*Sweeter than truth which aims at ill
Is falsehood, from a well-meant will.*

And

*When that the King doth counsel need,
Woe unto him who will mislead.*

4

II

On the porch of the Palace of Feridûn
was written what followeth :

*This life's show, my brother, endureth for
   none;*
*Give thy heart to the Maker of all things,
   alone;*
*To the kingdom of this world trust no-
   wise; 'twill glide*
*From thy grasp, as for others who dal-
   lied and died:*
*When the soul is a-flitting, what differ-
   ence is found*
*'Twixt the King on his throne, and the
   hind on the ground!*

III

One among the lords of Khorâsan saw
in vision Sultan Mahmûd Sebuktagin, a
hundred years after his death, when all
his body had mouldered into fragments
and become dust, excepting his eyes.

Those, as ever, moved about in their eyeholes, and darted their regards. All the Hakims were helpless at interpreting that dream, until a darweesh, making obeisance, said : " He goggles still, because some one else has got hold of his country."

Many a lord hath been shovelled away
Leaving no mark on his lands to-day;
Those proud old carcasses under the
* stones*
The grave hath eaten their last little
* bones;*
But the name of Nurshivan from year
* to year*
Lives, for his largesses, deathless and
* dear.*
O King, do good! fetch profit from
* breath,*
Before they say: 'Tis thine hour of death.

IV

OF a King's son I heard who was small in stature, and plain featured, whereas

6

his brothers were goodly in height and countenance. On a certain occasion his father, chancing to look at him with dislike and aversion, the son had insight to perceive this, and said, " Ah, my father ! a little man who is wise counts for more than a long man who is foolish. Not everything which is big is good."

Came it to your ears to hear
What the thin philosopher
One day, in his wisdom, said
To a proud, fat, pudding-head ?
"Friend !" quoth he, " an Arab steed
Though he should be lean indeed
By his quality surpasses
All a stableful of asses.

On this the King, his father, laughed, the pillars of the State approved, and the brothers were pricked to the heart.

While sword is sheathed and speech un-
spoken
Of valor or wisdom ye get no token ;

But call not the jungle empty—may be
A tiger sleeps there that ye did not see.

At that very time, as I heard, a formidable opponent made head against the King; and, the two armies coming face to face, the foremost to urge his steed towards the maidan of battle was that same dwarfed ugly Prince. Quoth he :

I am not one in the battle of whom they
shall see the back ;
Look for me where the blood runs thick
and the dust rolls black :
Leaders that flee from the field, with the
lives of their men make war ;
Stake your own souls on the fight ye who
the chieftains are !

With such words he assailed the enemy, and slew many warriors of renown. · When he returned to the King's presence he kissed the dust of obedience, and said :

Ye who judge by mere outsides
Heedless of what blemish hides,

8

Learn that in the battle-shocks
Lean horse helps, not fatted ox.

They say, moreover, that the soldiers
of the foe being many, and those of the
King few, a tayifah of the latter showed mind to fly, whereupon the young
Prince cried aloud : "*Ai Mardan!* bear
yourselves like men, or else put on
the clothes of women !" Hearing that
scornful speech the sowars regained
good heart, and, charging all together,
they obtained that day a great victory.

Afterwards the King kissed the head
and the eyes of his son, and folded him
to his bosom ; and, every day showing
him fresh kindness, finally appointed
him his *Wazir* and successor.

The brothers of the Prince, growing
envious, mixed poison with his food,
but his sister spied this from an upper
window, and closed the shutters with a
loud, warning noise, which signal he
comprehending, withheld hand from the
food, observing : "'Twere pity if the

wise should die, and fools should seek to take their place."

*If there were never a Homa-Bird to
    keep guard of kings,
Think ye for that that men would go
    under the gray owl's wings?*

Of all these things the King, his father, being informed, summoned the brothers, and having sternly rebuked them, banished each to a suitable corner of his kingdom, giving them the government there, in order that strife and jealousy might be removed, for as has been truly said:

*Ten darweeshes upon one mat sleep well
But in one kingdom two kings cannot
    dwell.*

And again:

*The man of God, with half a loaf to
    munch,
To fellow-beggars gives a broken hunch;
But if a king a whole dominion seizes
Till he take such another nothing pleases.*

V

A TAIFAH of Arab robbers had gathered on the top of a hill, and thence blocked the passage of caravans. The rayats of the district were sore troubled by their evil schemes, and even the force of the Sultan became baffled, because, having laid hands on a fortress upon the high ridge, they made it their habitual dwelling. Those who took counsel for that part of the country debated how such a trouble might be quickly removed, because, if suffered to continue, the extirpation of the robbers would become impossible.

A tree that to-day its first twig shoots
The hand of a little child lightly up-
　　roots,
But, if for a season ye shall delay
Oxen and cords will not drag it away;
With a straw may ye stop the springs, which drown
The lordly elephants lower down.

11

Their deliberations came to this—to
send forth some one to spy, who should
report a fair opportunity when the robbers would be absent plundering a tribe,
and when their lair would be empty.
Also they sent chosen men of understanding, tried in fight, who were to remain hidden in the pass under the hill.

At night when the freebooters returned from a raid, bringing their spoil
with them, they loosened their fighting
coats, and laid aside the loot ; and then
the first enemy that assailed them was
slumber, when a watch of the night had
passed.

The sun went down into Night's black
    valley
  As into their hungry maws the bread;
And as Yunus slid into the white whale's
    belly.
  *Each heavy eye sank into its head.**

The brave soldiers leaped from their

* An attempt to give the *double entendre* of
Sa'di's words.

hiding - place, and tied the wrists of all the robbers behind their backs. At dawn they brought them down into the Dargah of the King, who gave command to slay them one and all.

By chance there was among them a stripling whose youth had but just come to fruit. The fresh blossoms of the rose-garden of his cheeks were but newly opened. One of the Wuzeers kissed the footstool of the King's seat, and laying forehead of intercession upon the earth, said : "This boy hath not yet eaten any pomegranates from the orchard of life, nor tasted enjoyment of the sweetness of youth. My trust is, that in the com-passionateness of our lord's heart, he will forego the blood of this foolish one to me his slave, conferring thereby a great favor." At this the King wrin-kled his face with frowns, the thing not being conformable to his exalted under-standing, and he said :

In ever so good a soil the bad seed never will shoot,

Nuts may grow on a stone ere the worth-
less can come to fruit.

" Nay ! cut them off, tribe and scion
together ! It were better ! Tear them
up root and stalk ! To quench the fire
and leave the spark ; to slay the serpent
and spare its *butchas* is not the act of
the wise."

If the Water of Life were to rain
  The willows would bear ye no plums;
On the worthless bestow not your pain,
From the marsh-mallow no sugar comes.

The Wuzeer heard these words, and,
against his will, admired them, crying
" *Afrin !*" to the good sense of the King;
but observed : " What the Khudâwund
(may his kingdom be eternal !) has
deigned to let fall is absolutely true,
that had this youth continued in the
company of such wretches he too must
have become evil. But your slave is
hopeful that by the society of the upright the lad may obtain education and
the morals of the wise, being still only a

child; so that in the path of rebellion
and perverseness, such as those follow,
his feet cannot yet have become estab-
lished."

The wife of Lût, by wicked friends,
Brought all her house to shameful ends;
But in the Cave, with men of grace,
The Dog soon grew like Adam's race.

Thus spoke the Wuzeer, and a group
of the courtiers of the King made part
with him in pleading; so that his Majesty finally forewent his inclination for
the boy's blood, saying, " I pardon him,
albeit I do not see that it is right."

What Zal once said to Rustum, dost
  thou know?
Think none contemptible who is thy foe,
At fountain-head the rillet trickles small
Which, lower, drowns the camel, load
  and all.

In brief the Wuzeer took the youth to
his own house, and there nourished him
with favor and kindness. And a teacher,
a gifted man, was appointed to instruct

him in correct language and polite con-
versation, as well as in all the manners
of a court, so that he became approved
in the estimation of everybody. Once
the Wuzeer was speaking, in the presence of the King, about the lad's good
qualities and manners, and how the
teaching of virtuous people had taken
effect upon him, so that the old naughti-
ness had gone forth from his disposition,
at which the King laughed, and said:

The wolf's cub still a wolf will be
Though kept in saints' society.

Only two years afterwards a band of
runagates in his quarter of the city
joined with him, tying the knot of friendship, until that, at a time of opportunity,
he killed the Wuzeer together with his
two sons, carried off a vast amount of
booty, and, taking his father's place as
chief of the robbers of the cave, became
an arch offender like him. When they
told the King of all this he seized the
hand of astonishment in the teeth of in-
dignation, but remarked:

None forges from bad iron a good blade,
Nor—Oh, ye Hakims! is a villain made
Honest by teaching. The impartial rain—
Which falls on all alike—brings golden
　　grain
Forth of tilled fields, and from the gar-
　　den-plot
The tulip's beauteous cup. But waste
　　thou not
Seed on the sands that will no spikenard
　　grow;
He hurts the good who treats the wick-
　　ed so.

VI

A SERANG'S son I saw at the gate of
the Serai of Ughlumish who was en-
dowed with good sense, sagacity, information, and a perspicacity beyond all
praise. Even during his childhood the
marks of dignity were stamped upon his
forehead.

On his brow, with Wisdom bright,
Seemed to sit a star of Light.

B　　　　　17

Soon he grew well approved of the Sultan, because of his comely face and form, and great intelligence ; for the learned have said :

Worth not by wealth, but merit, gauge;
And wits by wise words, not by age.

His fellows grew envious of him, and falsely accusing him of treason, tried vainly to have him put to death, but

What can foe do
When friend stands true?

The King inquired : "Where is the reason of this jealousy against your state?" The young man replied : "Under the shadow of the greatness of my lord I have gained favor with all save the envious ones, whose only happiness would be in the decline of my good fortune. May the splendor and prosperity of my lord endure forever !"

I would not wound another's breast
But he that envies is possessed

Of self-made hurts. Die, ye who hate!
Since death alone from such estate
Can free you.
          Men of evil mind
Wish woe to all above them, blind
As bats are in the daylight. None
For that accuse the shining Sun!
Will ye hear truth? Better that such
     should pine
Blind by the thousand, than the Sun not
     shine.

VII

THEY tell a tale of one of the Kings
of Ajam, how he put forth the hand of
oppression over the goods of his raiyats,
and began a course of injustice and vexa-
tion, so that the people, under the tricks
of his tyranny, wandered afar into the
world, going on roads of separation, out
of distress at his evil rule. As the peas-
ants diminished in number the riches of
the country suffered loss, the treasury
grew empty, and enemies on all sides
brought up strength against him.

Whoso with help in storm would meet
Must bear himself in sunshine sweet;
The slave, his ring fixed in his ear,
Flees frightened, if ye make him fear;
Be gentle, generous; and so make
Strangers your slaves for kindness' sake.

One day in the Presence they were reading a book, the Shâhnâmeh, relating the downfall of the Kingdom of Zuhak and the reign of Feridûn. The Wuzeer put it to the King—why did Feridûn, without treasures, lands, or dignities, thus get the throne conferred upon him? The King replied: "Surely, as you have heard, the people drew to him by inclination, and, thus rendered strong, he became Padishah." "My lord," rejoined the Wuzeer, "if to gather subjects around one be the means towards gaining government, why dost thou scatter thine, unless it be that thou no longer desirest rule?"

As his own life a King his men should
cherish,
Without them power departs and king-
doms perish.

The King inquired : " What is the way to gather together soldiers and subjects?" The Wuzeer answered: "A Ruler must be just, so that men will assemble to him, and merciful, so that men may sit safe in shadow of his power ; and these two tokens have been absent from thee."

Tyrants their lordship cannot keep,
Nor wolves be shepherds to the sheep ;
Who rules by tyranny makes fall
The footstones of his kingdom's wall.

To the King the counsels of his Wuzeer, thus admonishing, did not recommend themselves. He commanded that they should bind him and cast him into prison. No long time elapsed before the sons of the King's uncle rose in arms and gathered an army, seeking to seize the sovereignty. And then many of those that had fled because of his oppressions joined the rebellion and gave it aid, so that the kingdom departed from that Sultan's possession.

Who tyrannizes those beneath his hand
In time of trouble finds his friends do
    stand
Strong on the foeman's side. Live sweet
    for all,
And then sit safely with an open wall;
Fear then no enemies ! A righteous King
Hath his realm round him like an iron
    ring.

VIII

A KING was sitting in a boat with a Persian slave, who had never before been upon the sea, nor borne the unpleasant motion of its waves ; consequently he fell to moaning and lamenting, and his whole body trembled with terror ; nor, however much he might be reassured, could anything give him tranquillity. The King's comfort was troubled by his outcry, and no remedy could be found. There was a Hakim in the boat who said : " If the Presence deign to order it I will put silence upon him." The King replied : " That would be the greatest kindness!" Thereupon the Hakim bade the crew cast the slave into the water. After he had undergone several sousings they seized his hair and dragged him to the end of the boat, where he clung with both hands to the rudder. On getting out he sate in a corner, and obtained tranquillity. Pleasure came to the King thereat. He asked: "What is the trick in this?" The Hakim replied: "Hitherto he had not tasted the true terror of plunging in the sea, nor known the real value of safety. In like manner he only understands how sweet is comfort who has been beforetimes plunged into misery."

Thou that art fat with feasting—what
*   to thee*
Is this my barley-loaf? She who to me
A Huri looks shows slut to wearier eyes,
And if a Huri were from Paradise
Exiled to 'Arâf that as Hell would seem,
While those in Hell would 'Arâf Heaven
*   deem.*

And again:

Who clips his mistress hath contentment
*   more*
Than he whose eyes watch for her open-
*   ing door.*

IX

THEY questioned King Hormuz, saying: "In the ministers of my lord's
father, what fault was discerned that he
should commit them to prison?" The
King replied: "I found no fault, but I
perceived that an excessive dread of me
was on their hearts, and that upon my
pledges they set no firm trust. I was
apprehensive, therefore, lest in fear of
injury to themselves they might try to
compass my destruction, so I adopted
the counsel of the Hakims, who have
said :"

Of him who fears thee stand afeared,
*   Albeit a hundred times more great ;*
The wild-cat at the leopard's beard
*   Darts, in her terror desperate ;*
Bites at the soldier's foot the snake
To save himself from stone and stake.

24

X

ONE of the Kings of the West had
fallen sick, being very old ; and all hope
of life was cut off from him, when suddenly a sowar entered at the gate and
brought good news that, by the might
of his lord's majesty, a certain fortress
had been taken, the hostile garrison captured, and sepoys, raiyats, and the rest
of the folk had all become obedient to
Government. Which when the King
heard, he heaved a mournful sigh, and
exclaimed: " This is not good tidings for
me, but for those who hate me—namely,
the successors to my kingdom."

*In one fond hope my foolish time has
  passed
Bethinking it should come to fruit at
  last ;
It comes ! but all too late to pluck !
  Death's day
Gives me my wish and takes my life
  away.*

The hand of Fate beats the departure-
drum :
Oh, my two eyes! the heavy hour is come ;
Say farewell to this head! Palm of my
hand
Take leave of wrist and arm! Nigh
me doth stand
Death, the fell master of all mortal
strife ;
Sweet friends, draw round me once again!
my life
Ends purposeless! I strove with folly;
nought
I did achieve! Be by my failure taught.

XI

ONE year I was making devotion by
the pillow of the tomb of the Prophet
Yahiya (*alayeh as salâm*, peace be upon
him !) in the Mosque of Damascus, when
a Prince of Arabia, infamous for his oppressions, came thither on a pilgrimage,
and performed the prayers, and made
supplications.

Rich ones and poor alike
Are bondsmen of the clay;
And they who most possess
Have most from Heaven to pray.

As he kneeled he turned his face towards me, and said: "For the reason that pure - mindedness is with Darweeshes, and that their ways are righteous, let thy spirit, I beg, go the same road with mine (in these prayers), because I live in fear of a powerful enemy." Then said I : "Show mercy to the humble, if thou wouldst not be in terror of the strong."

With iron arm and angry frown
'Tis base to push the poor man down;
Who pity not the weak, nor aid,
Shall find no help, being betrayed;
Who sow ill seed, and look to reap
Good fruit, a foolish fancy keep;
Pluck wool from ear, and justice grant,
That thou mayst hav't in hour of want.

Limbs of a body are we, sons of men,
Made from same clay, born of same
    origin ;

*When one limb suffers by misfortune's
    stress
Their fellows will not fare in happiness:
Thou, who unmoved canst others' sorrows
    scan
May be a monarch, but nowise a man.*

XII

A Darweesh, famed for the accepta-
tion of his prayers, arrived in Baghdad.
Hajaj Yusuf sent for him and said: "Pray
a good prayer for me!" The Darweesh
clasped his palms and cried: "O God!
take away this man's life!" Hajaj broke
forth: "O' God's name! what kind of
benediction is this?" The holy man answered: "A right good benediction for
thee and for all Mussulmans."

*Oh, heavy-handed Prince! scourge of the
    poor!
How long, think'st thou, shall earth's
    bazaar endure?
How long mak'st market of men's grief?
    Nay die!
Rid life of thee, and them of tyranny.*

XIII

AMONG unjust Kings was one who inquired of a holy man : "What form of service to Heaven were it best for me to perform?" He replied: "Sleep every day at noon ; for so doing, there will be a moment when thou wilt not be oppressing thy people."

That King I saw by day asleep,
And said: "'Tis good, slumber should keep
His evil eyes shut : but to die
Were better than, thus loathed, to lie !"

XIV

ONE lord I did hear spoken of who, having passed a whole night of pleasure, and being full-drunken, was singing :

Never to me came rosier hour than this,
Who care not whether good is, or bad is,
And let no meddler plague my perfect bliss.

But a Darweesh, who was sleeping naked in the snow outside, called aloud :

Oh, happy Prince ! of state unequalled—see,
'Tis well for you, but what say you of me ?

The King was tickled by this snatch, and flung a bag containing a thousand dinars out of the window, crying " Ho, Darweesh! hold up thy skirt!" To which the beggar replied : " How shall I hold up my skirt who have not a coat to my back ?" The Padishah, more and more compassionating his miserable state, made him the additional present of a garment.

In a little while that Darweesh ate up, or otherwise wasted, all his money, and came back. Wealth will not make long stay in the palms of holy men, nor patience in the hearts of lovers, nor water in a colander. They mentioned the beggar's return at a moment when the King was concerned with nothing so little, wherefore his Majesty became enraged, and turned away a frowning face.

In this respect those of sagacity and knowledge have warned us that we should be on our guard against the impatience and anger of Kings, who frequently have their minds full of important matters of state, and do not brook the burden of vulgar troubles.

Vainly the King's grace shall we seek
Who watcheth not fit time to speak;
Until speech find an open way
Be still—then fairly say thy say.

So the King cried, "Drive off this troublesome wastrel, who, in so brief a space, has squandered so much money! Teach him that the treasure of my *Bait-al-Mal* is to furnish a morsel for the hungry poor, not to glut the brother-hoods of Shaitan."

Who burns a torch by daylight—the man
of little wit—
Will have no oil for burning when lamps
at night are lit.

But one of the Wuzeers, a wise coun-cillor, spake: "Ai, Khudâwand! it seemeth proper that for such manner of folk fixed doles should be specially allotted, so that in the charges of daily need they may not exceed. But in that my lord hath commanded that such be altogether met with impediment and prohibition, this appeareth not suitable to the path pursued by lords of generosity, at one time causing the needy to be full of hopes by kindness, and at another by hopelessness, bursting his liver."

Admitted to the Presence by open door of grace,
No Prince may shut it hard again in any suppliant's face;
None sees the thirsty hadjis thronging the salt sea-shore,
Men, birds, and ants flock thither where the sweet spring pours its store.

XV

AMONG ancient Kings was one who in matters of rule lived negligent, and kept his army short of supplies. Accordingly, when a formidable enemy showed face against him his soldiers turned their backs.

Keep from a fighting-man his lawful pay,
And grudgingly on hilt his hand he'll lay.

One among those deserters was of my acquaintance. I loaded him with reproaches. I said it is base, unthankful, and contemptible if on account of any little difference of treatment a man turns away from an old master, forgetting the favors of many years. The soldier replied : " If I told you all, you would excuse me. How know you but that my horse went without barley, and that my *numdah* was in pawn?" A Prince who has gold and stints it to his troops, for the sake of such an one soldiers will not joyfully yield their lives.

Give the brave man his guerdon
Who risks for thee his skin,
Lest he shall turn offended
And a better master win.

C   33

XVI

THERE was a certain minister who, losing his post, found a company of Darweeshes, and the comfort of their society had the effect of bringing peace to his mind. At a later time the heart of his royal master grew again kindly towards him, so that he ordered him to be put back in office. But to this the Wuzeer was no longer willing to consent, saying that he had found disgrace better than employment.

They who in corner of retirement sit
'Scape mouths of rogues; by dogs are
*   never bit;*
Tearing the scroll, and laying down the
*   pen,*
No more they fear the tongues and hands
*   of men.*

The King said it is precisely a person of such wisdom that I lack for the management of my government; to which

the Wuzeer responded that the best
sign of such wisdom was for a man
not to give himself to any troublesome
labors.

The Homa-bird is honored all feathered
*   things above,*
Since harming nothing living, it feedeth
*   in the grove.*

They asked the black - eared lynx :
" Why dwell you as a slave with the lion ?
for what reason makst thou such a
choice ?" The lynx answered : " I eat
the leavings of my lion's hunting, and
from the fierceness of all enemies I live
safe under the shadow of the lion's
might."
Then they inquired of the Wuzeer :
" But now, since thou art beneath the
shadow of the King's protection, and
hast full conviction of his favor, why
not come nearer, so as to be one of the
circle of his trusted servants ?" The
Wuzeer replied : " I am not quite sure of
safety from the temper of my lion."

Though for a hundred faithful years the
Guebir feeds his flame,
Let him one moment fall therein, it burns
him all the same.

The courtier of a King may chance to
amass treasure, and may also chance to
lose his head. Sages have dwelt on the
dangers of this inconstancy of Princes,
who will sometimes be offended by com-
pliments, and sometimes will bestow a
Khilat for actual abuse. And they have
said : " Since wittiness, which is a need-
ful art in courtiers, is a defect in wise
men,"

Keep high and safe thy state of self-
command,
And leave their follies to the courtly
band.

XVII

ONE of my friends was bewailing to
me the hardness of the times, saying
how that he possessed such small means
and many children, and knew not how

to face penury. "Ofttimes, therefore,"
spake he, " it has entered my heart to go
into some other land, where, in whatever manner I might exist, information
about me, whether good or bad, would
come to no one."

Many with empty bellies have slept, and
nobody heeded their ache;
Many a soul hath come to the lips, and
no eyes wet for its sake!

" On the other hand, I am in dread of
the malignity of enemies, who will mock
at me behind my back and blame my
conduct, alleging that what I did for
the sake of my children was lack of manhood, saying : ' Look at that dishonored
one, who merits never to see again the
face of good fortune. For the sake of
his ease he leaves in misery his own wife
and children.' And, since in the art of
arithmic I have, as you wot, some little
skill—if, by your influence, any office of
court could be appointed to me, by
means of which tranquillity of mind

might return, the remainder of life would not suffice to express my gratitude."

"Oh, friend!" I answered, "the service of a King hath two aspects: the hope of bread, and the fear of death; and it is contrary to the counsel of the wise, for such a hope, to risk falling into such danger."

Nobody comes the Darweesh to rouse,
Crying,"Pay dues for garden and house!"
Make your account with woes to dance,
Or trust your guts, like the crow, to chance.

He said, "What you have observed does not apply to me, nor have you answered my question. Have you not heard how it has been declared that the hand of the man who practices dishonestly shakes as he renders his account?"

On honesty God's favor is bestowed,
I never saw one lost in a straight road.

The Hakims have also remarked that there are four persons who stand in deadly fear of other four: the murderer of the Sultan ; the thief of the constable ; the adulterer of the informer, and the harlot of the *muhtasib*. But by him whose account is clear at the rendering what fear needs to be felt ?

In office waste not, if thou will be free,
At quitting, from the stings of calumny :
Be just, then have no fear of any one,
'Tis the foul cloth the fuller bangs on
  stone.

Said I, " The story of that jackal exactly suits you, whom they saw running away at a gallop, and one cried out to him, " What catastrophe has befallen you so ?" The jackal panted forth, " I have heard that they are looking everywhere for camels, to put them to service." They replied, " Oh, fool ! what have you to do with camels, or camels with you ? What sort of likeness is there betwixt ye ?" He answered, " Khamoosh ! be silent ! for if any of the envious should cry, only for mischief's sake, 'This is a camel!' and I be seized, who, out of concern for my release, will demand investigation

39

of my case—and while the physic was being brought from Irak he who was bitten by the snake became dead."

Thus, too, as to yourself—albeit you are gifted with such moral excellence and integrity—there will be envious ones on the watch, enemies hiding round the corner ; and if, in regard to that beautiful conduct of yours, they should report something quite to the contrary, and on an evil occasion you come into the precincts of the King's wrath and fall under his displeasure, where will be the power of speech for you ? It seems to me far better for you to keep inside the Realm of Contentment, abandoning all perilous preferment, since the elect have remarked :

'Mid the deep sea are precious things in store,
But if you wish for safety stay ashore.

My friend, listening to these words, became angry, made a frowning face, and broke forth in accents of discontent: " What is there in all this of reason or adequacy, of understanding or conviction? It does but justify the saying of the Hakims, that 'in prison must one judge of friends, for sitting at meals all your enemies assume their appearance.'"

Reckon not him for a friend who, in good
  times, prates of his friendship,
Loads thee with brotherly love, boasts he
  will never deceive;
Friend I consider him only who, when ad-
  versity darkens,
Holds to his grip of thy hand, joys in thy
  grieving to grieve.

I noticed that he here became disturbed in temper, and regarded my counsel but as a hinderance. Moved thereby I repaired to a near friend, a Diwan, between whom and myself close intimacy had existed, and made representation of. my friend's circumstances to the minister, by reason of which a small preferment was conferred on him. Before many days had elapsed they discerned the amiability of his nature, and praised the excellence of his management. From that time forth matters prospered with him. He was advanced in rank—the star of his good fortune was in the ascendant, rising to the very meridian of his desires, until he even became a near favorite of the Sultan. At the deep contentment of his state I was rejoiced, and said :

Let go past troubles, have no more heart-
strife,
In depths of Darkness springs the Fount
of Life ;
Rail not at fickle Fortune ! Those who
eat
The fruit of bitter Patience find it sweet.

At that period it happened to me to go a journey to Mecca with a company of friends. When I was returning from my pilgrimage, he came out two stations to meet me. His outward appearance was of much distress, and he wore the look and dress of a Darweesh. "What is ill with thee?" I asked. "In the very manner," replied he, "which you foresaw. A party in the court took grudge against me, and made charge of treason about me; whereon the King willed not to seek the truth by close inquiry, while my old friends and my acquaintances— even the best—held silence in the matter of truth, forgetting all our by-gone intimacies."

When, by the Will of God, a man doth
*   fall,*
The world treads on his head—yea, one
*   and all;*
But when they see Luck take him by the
*   hand,*
With palms on breast round him the flat-
*   terers stand.*

In the end I was cast into prison with many indignities, until the present week, when arrived the glad tidings of the pilgrims' safe return. Then they set me free from my cruel bonds, but deprived me of my family estates. Truly the service of the Padishah is like a voyage upon the sea : profitable yet perilous. Either we gain the treasure, or we perish in the buffeting waves. Ah—yes!

43

With ruddy gold in both his palms the
*   merchant comes to land,*
Or else the waves, some bitter day, roll
*   him upon the sand.*

I had no mind, at this, to probe his
bleeding inner wounds, or to rub salt
into them, and therefore cut short what
I had to remark into these two "baits."

What! knew ye not that those will see
*   upon their feet the chain*
Into whose ears good counsel comes but
*   to go forth again?*
Another time, if scorpion's sting to bear
*   your powers fail,*
Put not a foolish finger in hole of "Cur-
*   ly-tail."*

XVIII

In my fellowship were once certain holy
persons, whose outward behavior appeared to be adorned with rectitude, so
that one of our principal men had an ex-
cellent opinion of them, and allotted a
regular stipend for their support. But a

certain member of the company happen-
ing to do something thought unbecom-
ing in Darweeshes, that good opinion became adversely changed, and the market
of favor was shut against them all.   I
wished, if possible, to obtain a restitu-
tion of the allowance for my acquaintances, and resolved to pay my respects,
in that view, to the great man.   But the
door-keeper shut the gate upon me, with
much incivility, which I forgave, because
it has been remarked :

If to the gate of Wuzeer, Mîr, or Prince,
You go unrecommended, hurry thence !
Dog and Door-keeper, when they see you
     poor,
Drag you by skirt or collar from the door.

But as soon as the servants of his
Highness better understood my position,
they gave me entrance with all respect,
and offered me a superior waiting-place.
I, however, took in all humility a lower
seat than that assigned—observing, as
runs the *bayt :*

Excuse me; slave I am—not fit,
Except in bandah-khan to sit !

One exclaimed : " Allah, Allah ! what
reason is there to speak thus ?"

Sit where thou wilt ! Sit on my head, my
eyes !
We know thee gallant, worthy—past dis-
guise.

So I sate me down and joined in various topics of talk, until the story of the
abasement of my friend came into mention, when I cited this *Ki'ta :*

What fault beyond forgiving did our
high lord discern,
That from a faithful servant he should
so harshly turn ?
Alas ! to God only pertains the greatness
of such grace
As marks the slip, yet not for that
averts the pardoning face.

Being reported to the Presence, these
words pleased, and it was commanded
that the means of subsistence should be

restored to my friend, and that, in the manner of the past, they should prepare his daily food, allowing for the interval of intermission. As for me, I thanked the Prince for such favor, kissing the dust of service, and excusing the boldness of my plea; while, at the moment of dismissal, I spoke this *Ki'ta:*

*To Mecca's holy Kibleh men turn them
    when they pray,
And journey thither many a league, o'er
    many a weary way;
So must my lord be patient with those
    that importune—
We pelt the loaded fruit-tree, but fling
    not at the moon.*

XIX

THERE was a Prince's son, who inherited from his father a prodigious patrimony. He spread wide the hand of liberality, bestowing countless bounties and gifts on his sepoys and subjects. What saith the *Ki'ta?*

47

There issueth naught of odor from teb-
    lahs piled with spice,
But freely burn it in the flame, and fra-
    grance shall arise !
Wouldst thou be praised for bounty?
    bestow with might and main ;
Seed scattered grows to harvest, and not
    the hoarded grain.

One among the courtiers lacking dis-
cretion began to give advice, saying how
the King's ancestors had gathered together all their treasure by strenuous
efforts and with a view to some hour of
need. "Therefore," said he, "withdraw
thy hand from such action, lest when
events press thee in front and enemies
attack thee behind, thou be found destitute in the face of danger. Even though
one should squander the whole wealth
of the state upon the multitude, every
householder would not thus receive more
than a grain of rice. Far better to take
from each of them a grain of silver, which
would accumulate for thee day by day
into vast resources."

At this speech the Prince frowned, because it was not conformable to his feelings, and he said, " The Lord of all Glory and Majesty hath made me King in order that I should occupy and distribute, not that I should behave like a mere watchman of treasure, for there runneth a verse :"

Karûn, with forty chambers full of gold,
None names : Nowshirwan's name never
grows old.

It is recorded how that Nowshirwan, who was called " The Just "—being at his Shikargahi a-hunting—was for having some roasted game, but there was no salt. A slave was therefore sent to the village to fetch some salt, with money to pay for it, so that such a demand might not become customary and the villagers be impoverished. They said to him,"Oh, my lord ! from such a trifle how could any injury occur?" The Prince rejoined: " The beginning of injustice in the world came by little wrongs, which every new tyrant hath since made bigger, un-

til we have ended in monstrous oppressions; as saith that verse:"

*If from the garden of the poor the King
    eats one small fruit,
His slaves will take occasion the whole
    tree to uproot;
If he shall seize five eggs to make a dish,
    not paying cost,
The people of his camp will spit a thou-
    sand fowls for roast.*

And again:

*An end comes to the proud oppressor's
    state,
But no end to the people's curse and hate.*

XX

I KNEW of an Omlah, a gatherer of revenues, who ruined the dwellings of the
raiyats in order that the treasure-cham-
ber of the Prince, his master, might be
full, unmindful of the decree of the wise,
which hath said: "Whosoever sinneth
against the Most High, in order to gain

the favor of mortal man—God the Almighty will turn against him, making that very mortal to become during life his destruction."

*Flames in the wild dry rue no such
    smoke make
As mounts, in smoke of sighs, when sad
    hearts break.*

They say the lion is the chief of all beasts, and the ass the meanest, yet—by agreement of wise men — the ass carrying his load is better than the lion devouring men.

*The lowly ass, that hath no wit,
Bearing his load is blest for it;
Pack-cattle at their patient toil
Count more than rogues who vex and
    spoil.*

And the King, becoming informed of some among the tax-gatherer's wicked acts, caused him to be stretched on the *shikanjah*, and by various modes of torment put him to death.

The King's love he shall best attain
Who first his subjects' hearts can gain;
Wilt thou have God be good to thee,
From harshness to His creatures flee!

One who had had experience of the man's cruelties passed nigh to him at the hour of doom, and remarked :

Not all—I see!—because of might un-
* hallowed,*
Can safely make the poor man's state
* accurst;*
The throat may gulp the bone, but—be-
* ing swallowed—*
'Twill bulge the navel, and the belly
* burst.*

XXI

OF a ruffian soldier they relate a tale, how he once flung a rock at the pate of a Darweesh. The holy man, unable to revenge the affront, kept the stone to himself, until a time when the Malek, being incensed against this *lashkari*, ordered him to be cast into a pit. Thither

came presently the Darweesh and threw
the stone at the soldier's head. The
man said, "Who art thou? and why dost
thou hurl this stone at my head?" Quoth
the Darweesh, "I am such and such an
one, and that stone is the very same
which on a certain day thou didst fling
at me!" The soldier said, "And all
this while long, why didst thou wait?"
Answered the Darweesh, "At that time
I was afraid because of thy calling, but
seeing thee in the pit, I counted the
present a fortunate opportunity."

When strong and rich the wicked ones
*   you see,*
'Tis good to live resigned, and let them
*   be:*
Not having nails to tear away their
*   eyes,*
The least of fighting is the most of
*   wise:*
Who grapples against an arm of iron
*   breaks*
His own wrist — were it silver. Pru-
*   dence makes*

*The cautious wait, till Fate their
strength constrains,
Then—to the joy of all—dash out their
brains.*

XXII

A CERTAIN King was afflicted with a
disease so horrible that to give description of it would not be proper. A number of foreign physicians agreed that no
remedy existed for this except the gall
of a male child who had certain especial
bodily marks. The King commanded
search to be made for such an one, and
he was found in the son of a raiyat,
bearing all the qualities prescribed. The
King summoned the father and mother,
and, by boundless largesses, purchased
their assent—while his kazi also issued a
fetwa that to spill peasant's blood for
the purpose of restoring health to his
Majesty would be an eminently lawful
thing.

The *Jallad* (executioner) was prepar-
ing to despatch the youth, when he lifted

his face towards heaven, and laughed. The King asked : " What can there possibly be in thy present situation that thou shouldest laugh ?" The boy replied: "Affection children expect from their father and mother ; a private wrong they carry to the kazi ; and they look for justice from their sovereign. In my case my father and mother, for the sake of paltry worldly profit, have given me over to slaughter ; my protector, the kazi, has decreed me to die, and the Sultan hopes for his own recovery only by my murder. Except in Almighty God I possess no refuge."

Where elsewhere look? when my sad
    plaint is laid
'Gainst King, judge, parents — by them
    all betrayed.

At these words the King's heart grew troubled, and the water came into his seeing. " Better it were," spake he, " for me to die than to shed the blood of the innocent." Therepuon he kissed the head

and eyes of the lad, and embraced him,'
and gave him splendid presents, and let
him go free. Moreover, they say that
the Malek quite recovered his health
that same week. And this gives to think
of what a *pil-bân* * remarked on the
banks of the River Nile :

To know how the little ant doth feel
Under thy pitiless passing heel,
Lie in the elephant's path thou must,
And let his great foot crush thee to dust.

XXIII

UMROOLEESH had among his slaves
one who ran away from service, and the
people who went after and captured him
having brought him back, the minister
of the Prince, feeling ill-will against the
fugitive, ordered him to be put to death.
The slave placed his head on the earth
before the Prince, and said :

* *Mahoot*, elephant-driver.

*Whatever falls, falls justly, if ordered by
the King,
The slave against his lord's behest utters
not anything.*

"But," continued he, "since I have
been nourished under the glories of this
royal house, I am loath that on the judg-
ment-day my lord shall be charged with
my blood. If you desire to have your
slave slain, do it, in fine, with just obedience to the law. Kill me so that, at the
resurrection, you may not be called to
account."

The King made answer : "What obedience can I render to the law?" The
slave replied : "Grant permission that I
kill your minister, and then, in revenge
of him, order me to be put to death, so
that I may be justly executed." At this
the King in turn laughed, and, turning
to the Wuzeer, asked what advice he
would deem proper to offer? His Excellency responded: "Ai Khudawand !
set free this rascal I pray, as a sacrifice
at the tomb of thy fathers, so that I also

may not be caused to fall into misfortune.
On my part is the fault, who did not
bear in mind the weighty words of the
Hakims, that have said :"

When with a clod-thrower thou wagest
fight
Expect a miry game;
When thou hast shot thy shaft in foe-
man's sight,
Sit where he cannot aim !

XXIV

THE King of Zazan had an agent of
kindly nature and goodly bearing, who
was courteous to all alike coming into
his presence; and in their absence spoke
equally well of all.   By chance some act
of his was found unpleasing in the sight
of the Prince, who fined him and ordered
him to be punished.   His Majesty's *sar-*
hangs, holding themselves bound by
former favors to be grateful to their
prisoner, during the period of his captivity showed him politeness and consid-

eration; and prohibited any harsh treatment or severity.

Peace with an enemy if you desire,
Praise him the more he blames: let
him be bitter;
At last in malice even the worst must tire.
Make your mouth sweet, and his will
not be bitter.

Of what caused the anger of the King, some few things were by inquiry cleared away; but for others he still remained in prison. One of the neighboring lords of the region secretly sent him a message, saying: "High personages in thy vicinity have, alas! not known the worth of thine Excellency, and have done thee dishonor. If the disposition of one so noble (Allah prosper all thy future undertakings!) be well-disposed towards our service, we will entreat him well in paying regard to his deserts in all possible ways, since those in authority here would be rejoiced in welcoming him, and now await his answer."

The agent received and understood

this; and, recognizing his peril, wrote the reply which he judged fit on the back of the same letter, duly returning it. One of the King's *mutàallakîn* came to know of these matters, and informed his Majesty, saying : " A certain one, whose imprisonment the Presence commanded, holds intercourse by letter with great persons of the neighborhood." The King grew very angry and ordered search to be made ; so they seized the *Kâsid*, and read the despatched letter which he was carrying. Thus was it written on the back : "The gracious opinion of the great senders far exceeds all merit of their lowly servant, but any acceptance of the honor proffered is not in possibility, forasmuch as, having been provided for by the bounty of my lord's household, I cannot—for a little change in the mind of my good master — show towards him traitorous ingratitude. Hath it not been declared ?"

Against thy lover bear it not in mind
If once, or twice, in life he prove unkind.

With the King this high sense of right was very well accepted. He bestowed rich presents and a Khilât upon the agent, and craved his forgiveness, saying: "I have committed a fault: I have wrought unkindly with thee who hast done no wrong." That one answered, "Aye! Khudâwand! your servant permitteth not himself to see any fault of his lord herein; but being as it was the *takdir* of Allah that some calamity should befall me, best happened it coming by that hand from which in past days so many favors and benefits and so much grace have descended."

If by mankind misfortunes seem to fall
  Rail not! they cannot make thee joy
    or woe;
Know that from God alone—Who governs
  all—
Proceed these contraries of friend and
  foe.
From bowstring starts the shaft, but,
  who is wise,
Looks to the bowman to learn why it flies.

XXV

ONE of the Western Kings commanded the officers of his Diwân to increase
the pay of a certain person, because
he was always faithful to his orders,
while the other attendants were given
to play and dissipation, neglecting their
duties. A lord of judgment heard this
and remarked: "The high degrees of
service in the Durgâh of divine glory and
power are in the same way obtained."

*Who serves for two dawnings with duty
    his King
Will win the third morning those glances
    that bring
Contentment and favor. True worship-
    pers know
They shall not unhopeful from Allah's
    face go.*

*By dutifulness greatness grows; the way
To diminution is to disobey:
Those who the forehead of good fate will
    owe
On threshold of fair service lay it low.*

XXVI

OF an unjust person they record a story, how he was wont to buy hezum-fuel from the poor at unfair prices, and sell it to rich folks at their own fancy. A perceptive man, walking by his shop, said :

*Snake! that at every passing heel dost
    bite!*
*Owl! that dost foul wherever thou
    dost perch!*
Albeit thy sins may now evade the light,
*They shall not Allah's searching
    judgment lurch;*
*Quit thine oppressions of earth's feeble
    poor,*
*That to the sky their curses mount no
    more.*

The unjust dealer, incensed at these words, turned a frowning countenance upon the speaker, and cherished ill-will against him, until one night, when flames from the kitchen (*matbakh*) caught upon the pile of his firewood, and burned up all his goods, out of his comfortable bed making a heap of ashes. It chanced that the sagacious one came by at that very time and overheard the dealer saying to his friends : "I know not whence these flames have sprung to seize upon my *serai.*" Whereat the wise man exclaimed, "From the fire of the burning hearts of the poor they came !"

Beware of the smoke that from souls doth
  part,
  For the flame will burst from the
  ashes at length !
Wrong not too deeply one human heart,
  For a sigh to o'erturn the world hath
  strength !

Have in mind what was written upon the diadem of Shah Kaikhosran :

Throughout what years, what ages, men
  will tread—
Crowned now, but covered then with dust
  —this head,
This diadem, passed to me, brow by brow,
Others must wear it as I wear it now.

XXVII

A CERTAIN person in the art of wrestling had reached the very top. Three hundred and sixty different grips and falls did he know—all good—and every day would show off some fresh sleight. Having a special corner of his heart for one among his pupils, a handsome youth, he taught him three hundred and fifty-nine out of his tricks, but kept the knowledge of the last one from him. The young man thus became first among all rivals in skill and strength, and none of them could at all cope with him. To such a pitch, in consequence, rose his vanity that before the Sultan himself he said: " The superiority of my master over me is that which I allow to him on account of his age, and because he has educated me; otherwise in point of strength I am not his inferior, and in point of skill I am his equal." The Sultan did not like this departure from reverence on the youth's part, and commanded that there should be held a

wrestling-match between them. An open
spot was selected; those columns of the
country, the ministers, and those eyes
of Majesty, the nobles, were all present,
when the youth, like an elephant in
"wust," strode into the ring, showing a
force which seemed as though it could
move a mountain of iron.

The teacher, who well knew that his
pupil was now of greater bodily force
than himself, laid hold of his adversary
with that cunning clinch which he had
withheld in his instructions; and the
youth, being ignorant how to encounter
it, was lifted with both hands by the
Master high above his head, and dashed
upon the earth. Shouts arose from the
spectators : as for the Sultan, he directed that a robe of honor and presents in
money should be given to the teacher,
while he rebuked and derided the young
man, saying : "Thou didst rudely dare
to put thyself in competition with him
who made thee, and thou hast shame-
fully failed."

The defeated man muttered : "Aye,

Khudâwund! my master did not prevail over me by strength, nor yet by
science, but because there remained one
little secret of his art which he would
not impart, and by that slight thing he
hath got the upper hand of me." "Aye,"
said the teacher, "on account of such
a day as this I kept it back, for the wise
have remarked, 'not even to a friend
allow so much advantage, as that, some
day becoming an enemy, he may hold
you in his power.' Heard ye never the
verse about him who suffered wrong
from the very one whom he had nourished and brought up?"

Either fidelity's no more afoot,
  Or none doth practise it on earth be-
    low:
I never taught a young hand how to
    shoot,
  But, in the end, at me he drew his
    bow.

XXVIII

A Darweesh, living all alone, was sitting in a desert spot. The Sultan passed that way; but the Darweesh, for the reason that freedom from desires is in itself a kingdom of contentment, did not so much as lift up his head, nor show the smallest attention. On this the Sultan, full of the glory of his kingdom, grew wroth and said: "Truly these rag-wearing folks have only the manners of brute beasts!" Whereon the Wuzeer of the Sultan said to the man: "My lord, who is lord over the face of all the earth, passed but lately by thee! Why mad'st thou no humble obeisance, nor perform'dst even ordinary salutations of reverence?" The beggar replied: "Tell thy King to set his expectation of reverences on such as hope to receive favor and profit from him, and bid him also know that Kings are created for the care-taking of their people, and not the people for prostrating themselves to the Kings."

The King is sentry for the poor
Despite of power and wealth in store;
Not for the shepherd are the sheep,
The shepherd hath the flock to keep.

To-day this one is prosperous, and that
  a stricken slave;
Wait for a while, till earth has eat
  the brains of fool and knave,
Then shall be seen what difference sur-
  viveth 'twixt those two—
King's majesty, slave's misery — when
  Fate's full scroll comes true.
Open the tombs and see the bones there
  mixed in mockery!
Which dust was servant, which was
  lord's?—open the tombs, and see!

To the King the speech of the Darweesh seemed of sturdy sense. He said :
"Ask whatever thou wilt from me."
The man replied, "I ask that thou wilt
not further trouble me!" Quoth the
Sultan, "Well, then, give me some of thy
counsel!" The beggar responded with
this verse :

69

Bethink ye, Kings! while lordly and
opulent ye stand,
Kingdoms, and gold, and sceptres must
pass from hand to hand.

XXIX

An officer of state appeared before
Zûlnûn of Egypt, and sought encour-
agement from him, saying : "Night and
day I am occupied in the service of my
lord, hoping reward from his liberality,
and dreading punishment from his displeasure." Sultan Zúlnûn wept, and said :
"If I had only been to Allah, as thou to
thy master, by this time I were high
among the elect !"

From hope of Heaven and fear of Hell
if piety were free
The feet of all the Darweeshes in Heaven
would planted be :
And if the Wuzeer dreaded God as he
doth fear the King,
With archangels of Paradise that man
might soar and sing !

XXX

A PADISHAH gave command to put an innocent person to death. He said: "Aye, Malek ! by reason of your wrath against me inflict not on yourself an injury !" "In what way?" asked the King. The man replied, "This torment will cease ·for me with my breath, but the sin of it will endure upon you for ever and ever."

Like the breath of the desert time pass-eth away,
Glad and sad—fair and foul—all condi-tions decay :
The tyrant bethought to wreak evil on me,
It rides on his own neck, and mine goeth free !

The King profited by the counsel; desisted from inclination for the man's blood, and prayed his forgiveness.

XXXI

THE state officers of Nowshîrwan were busy one day in considering some great affair of the kingdom, and each, to the extent of his understanding, was delivering his opinion. The King also, in like manner, expressed a judgment. Bazer - chameher, when his turn came, declared himself for the view of his Majesty. The ministers asked him, in private, "What superiority didst thou discern in the opinion of the Sultan over those of so many sagacious councillors?" He answered : "Seeing that the issue of a business is never known beforehand, and that all judgments must be judged by the pleasure of Allah the Most High, whether they be right or wrong, therefore accordance with the opinion of the King is the best course. Then, if things go amiss, on account of my deference my error shall surely escape blame."

*In counsel 'gainst the wish of Kings to
    stand
Is in a man's own blood to wash his hand;
If he shall call the broadest daytime Night
Say " Yea, Sire ! Moon and Planets swim
    in sight !"*

XXXII

ONE who was a pretender, and had twisted his hair in ringlets, as being of Ali's line, coming into the city with the Kafilah from Hedjaz, gave himself out as a Hadji returning, and laid a thesis before the King, saying that it was of his own composition. Among the King's attendants was one just arrived from journeying, who remarked, " I saw this man at the Eed of Uzrah in Bassora; how then can be be a Hadji?" Another observed, " His father was a Nazarani of Mallatee ; how then can he be of the line of Ali?" As for his verses, they presently found those in the Diwan of Anwarî.

The King commanded that they should beat him and drive him away, first asking him why he had uttered so many lies. He answered, " Ai, Khudâwand ! lord of the face of the earth ! one thing more will I say, which if it be not true, then, in whatever way you order, I shall indeed deserve punishment." "What thing is that?" quoth the King. He replied:

You ask for butter-milk: the dealer brings
  Drink two parts water, and one spoon-
    ful, sooth;
Be not so angered with your slave who
    flings
  Some travellers' lies into his bowl of
    truth!

The King laughed and said: "Thou hast never spoken more truly!" and directed them to allot him the *ma'mul* customary for his class.

XXXIII

THEY relate how a certain person of state, who had borne himself merciful to those beneath him, and sought harmony and peace with each, came by chance into the Sultan's displeasure. Then did all those others spend endeavors in obtaining his release; while his guards, during his imprisonment, were gentle towards him; and many great ones along with the rest spoke so well of his virtue to the King that at last his Majesty overlooked the offence.

One of good parts, hearing these circumstances, observed:

The hearts of friends your own to make
Burn down a father's garden! Break
The house up! All its chattels spoil
To set a friend's pot on the boil!
Be kind to rogues and slanderers—
Sweet morsels shut the mouths of curs.

XXXIV

HAROUN-AL-RASHÎD had a son who came once into his father's presence, highly enraged, saying that the son of a certain Sarhang had used words of abuse about his mother. Haroun asked those pillars of the state, his ministers, what was a befitting penalty for such an offence. One was for the man's execution; another suggested cutting out his tongue; and yet another proposed to fine and banish the culprit. But Haroun said : "Oh, my son! punish him with pardon—that is best! and if thou art not able to be so great, then do thou in turn abuse his mother, yet not so rudely that—*intigâm* —vengeance should pass beyond limits, since so the injury would be wrought by our side!" It is written :

Not so much man—the wise declare—
Is he who brings wild beasts to war,
As he, who even in anger's heat,
Utters no words which are not meet.

And again :

An ill-conditioned fellow railed amain,
A wise one took't with thanks: "Sir!
*   why complain*
Of aught you say? I am much worse
*   than so,*
If you knew all my faults, as I them
*   know !"*

XXXV

I was on board a ship with people of quality, when, close at hand, a shallop became capsized, and two fishermen—

brothers — fell into the broken water.
One of my company cried to a sailor,
"Lay hold of those two and save them,
and I will give you a hundred dinârs !"
The sailor made efforts and rescued one
of the two; the other perished by drown-
ing. I remarked : "There was no destined remainder of his life left ; for that
cause delay took place in getting hold
of him." The Mallâh (sailor) smiled,
and replied : "That which thou sayest
is correct, but, beside this, my own inclination to help the man I saved was
stronger, because, on a certain day, when
I was very weary in the desert he put me
upon his camel, while from the hand of
the lost man I got the *tâziyânah* — the
whip — in the days of my childhood."

Vex no man's secret soul—if that can be—
The path of life hath far too many
  a thorn !
Help whom thou may'st — for, surely —
  unto thee
Sharp need of help will—e'er the end
  —be borne.

XXXVI

Two brothers there were: one did service for the Sultan, and the other by the labor of his hands ate daily bread. The richer brother once asked of the poorer, " Why do you not take his Majesty's employ, so as to be freed from the abjectness of toil?" whereat the poor one said, " And why dost thou not work, in order to be relieved from the disgrace of dependency?" For the Hakims remark that "to sit and eat one's own bread is better than standing on duty with a golden girdle, while —service for service."

Better be plasterer, using thy hands mixing the quick and the slack,
Than to cross those hands on a hireling's breast—a slave at the Amir's back.

And again:

Ye waste the days of your lifetime, thinking with care and fear
" What shall we eat in the summer, in winter what shall we wear ?"

78

Aye, shikam! Ignoble belly! Content
thyself with a cake,
Lest thy better, the manly backbone, with
shameful bending should break.

XXXVII

SOMEBODY brought as glad tidings to Nowshîrvan, the Just, news that the God of all Majesty had been pleased to remove by death one of his antagonists. The Sultan inquired: "Have you by chance heard, then, that God means to exempt from such a fate thy master?"

To know mine enemy is dead hath nought
of joy for me,
Only I learn the lesson that I shall be
as he.

XXXVIII

A CABINET of ministers, at the court of Kisra, were talking together upon an affair of state; and, Bazarchemeher remaining silent, they inquired why he uttered no word in the discussion. He replied : "Wuzeers are made in the fashion of physicians, and your *tabîb*, the doctor, administereth not physic save to the sick. Therefore, so long as I observe your counsels going judiciously, for me to speak a single word would be unwise."

When work moves well, the less that's
  said
  Is so much gain—I bide my time;
But if I see the blind man led
  Straight to the pit, silence were crime.

XXXIX

HAROUN-AL-RASHÎD, when the land of Egypt had been subdued by him, made proclamation : " In order to shame that rebel who, in the pride of possessing the Kingdom of Misr, boasted himself to be God, I will bestow this throne of Egypt on the very meanest of my slaves." And he gave it, indeed, to a dull-witted Ethiopian black, whom he owned, named Khusaheb. As to the wisdom and sense of this man, they relate that when a band of cultivators made complaint to him that their cotton, sown on the banks of the Nile, had been ruined by untimely rain, he replied, "The proper thing for you to do then is to sow wool." A wise man, hearing this, remarked :

If wealth did wax with wisdom, fools
  Would all die hungry. But God gives
Such bounty to his fool as serves
  To feed a hundred wiser lives.
Fortune and wealth come not by wit
  Save when Heav'n wills. It doth befall
The silly ones win dignities,
  The worthy ones go to the wall.
Seeking for gold the alchemist died poor,
The fool found plenty under an old door.

F

XL

Iskander the Grecian was asked: "By what means didst thou occupy so many realms of East and West, seeing that monarchs before thee, with larger treasure, vaster territories, riper years, and more numerous troops, did not achieve such conquests?" The great victor replied, "Whenever, by the favor of the Gods, I subdued a kingdom, I abstained from oppressing its inhabitants, and never named the names of their Kings without words of respect."

Him great the wise will never style
Who of great men utters things vile.

And again :

These all are nought, after their hour—
Treasures and crowns, command and
   power,
Possession, conquest, victory.
Yet let no dead be blamed by thee
Who greatly lived, that thou may'st have
A lasting name even in thy grave.

82

THE GULISTAN

OR

ROSE-GARDEN

OF

SHAIKH SA'DI

Gateway the Second
CONCERNING DARWEESHES

CONCERNING DARWEESHES

___

I

ONE of the great ones asked a pious man what was his opinion about a certain devotee of whose moral character people had spoken disparagingly. He answered, "In his outward appearance I perceive no fault, and as to what is concealed within him I know nought."

Whom in holy clothes you see
Take him holy man to be;
What he hideth let him hide,
Mohtesibs * step not inside.

* Police inspectors.

II

A Darweesh I once saw at Mecca, who, with his forehead laid against the Kiblah, was moaning and praying : "*Ya, Ghafûr!* Oh, thou that pardonest! *Ya, Raheem!* Oh, Thou that art merciful! Only Thou knowest what is fit to be uttered or offered to Thee, can go forth from me, the most sinful and ignorant of men! I say not forgive me the faults of my service, for I have not served nor obeyed. They who know Thee, and have offended, ask and obtain pardon for their imperfections. The devout claim reward for their devotion, as merchants take the price of their trading stock. I, thine unworthy slave, have brought Thee not my piety but my hope — I am come hither to beg, not to bargain!"

Whether 'tis death or mercy, my face and forehead I lay
Here at thy holy threshold. A slave must hear and obey!

Yea! I heard that poor but wise men-

dicant at the gate of the Ka'aba, bitterly
weeping, and crying sweetly :

*Oh, God, I say not hear my prayers! I say
Blot with forgiving pen my sins away!*

III

ABDUL KÂDUR GILANÎ, also, lay with
his face upon the dust before the sacred
enclosure of the Ka'aba at Mecca, and
what he said was "Ai, Khudâwand !
grant me pardon !—but if I may not be
pardoned, then, at the Judgment, raise
me up blind, so that I shall not stand
ashamed in the presence of the righteous."

*Head in the dust, with contrite heart,
    when morn brings sense I say,
"Oh, God! of Whom I ever think, think
    Thou of me to-day!"*

IV

A THIEF effected entrance into the
abode of a pious man ; but for all the

searching he made could not lay hands upon a single article of worth, and he therefore grew sorely troubled in spirit. Knowledge of this coming to the pious man, he threw the *gilîm* on which he himself was sleeping in the pathway of the robber, so that he should not return wholly disheartened.

I heard that men who walk God's way
Not even to foemen ill things will say;
How canst thou reach this noble height
Who with thine own dost wrangle and
    fight?

The goodness of upright men is the same in presence and in absence — not like the false sweetness of those who abuse you behind your back, and to your face protest themselves ready to die for you.

As meek as lambs if there be fear,
Savage as wolves when they can tear.

He who recounts to thee faults of thy
    brothers
Hastens to tell thy faults, too, to the others.

88

V

A COMPANY of people were travelling
together, sharing the pleasures and
troubles of the journey. I had a wish to
join them, but they withheld their consent. At this I said it was not comform-
able with the manners of worthy persons
to turn away their faces from companionship with the necessitous, and to deny the
advantage of society, the more so as I
could profess myself to be of a spirit to
make an useful friend and no mere burden of their hearts. One among them,
however, replied : "Take not too much
to heart our refusal, because not long
ago a person, habited as a Darweesh—but
a thief in reality — threaded himself on
the string of our association."

*How can one guess what man a garment
   hides ?*
*The scribe knows what he writes — and
   none besides.*

"And since the state of a Darweesh
should be good and trustworthy, we

did not suspect, but admitted him to our number."

The Darweesh dons his woollen shroud
And shows religious to the crowd,
But body may—if heart be right—
Wear what it will, a diadem bright,
Or cap of felt. 'Tis not their dress
Makes saints! Wear satin, and sin
*   less!*
Holiness comes by holy deeds,
Not starving flesh of daily needs.
In padded coats the soldiers fare,
But eunuchs want no arms of war.

" Briefly we had been journeying until nightfall, and, when darkness fell, lay down at the foot of a hissar, at which time that graceless thief, taking the water-pot of one of our companions, and saying that he was going for his occasions, set forth to steal."

If such an one were holy for his garb of
*   piety,*
The veil that drapes the Ka'aba an ass's
*   rug might be.*

"As soon as he was gone clear from the sight of us Darweeshes, and became concealed, he climbed into a tower and stole a box. By the time daylight was abroad, the black-hearted wretch had fled afar off, and we, his unoffending associates, who were sleeping quietly, were seized and carried into the castle, and cast into dungeons. From that time we have determined to avoid companionship and to pursue the road of retirement. If any in a company commits folly, there is no difference made between the better and the worse among them. Have you not seen how a single mad cow will lead the herd astray?"

"Truly!" I replied; "but, thanks to the God of all Majesty and Glory, I shall not be quite deprived of the benefit of the wisdom of Darweeshes, albeit I am to be debarred from their holy society, for I have gathered admonition from this story which will be of utility to men of my kind all the days of our lives."

In the chaplet of good conduct one stone
    blemished spoils it all;
Tanks of rose-water grow filthy if a
    dog thereinto fall.

VI

THERE was a Zahid who was guest of a
Sultan. While they sat at the cloth he
ate less than was his wont, and when
they rose for the Namâz he prayed
longer than was usual, so that the opinion of his temperance and piety might
be increased.

Oh, Arab man! the Ka'aba meseems
    thou'lt never see!
It is the road to Turkestan* is travelled
    now by thee.

When he was come back to his own
place he bade the table be brought that
he might take food. His son, a youth
of penetration, said: "Oh, father! Did

* Country of infidels.

you not eat anything, then, at the Sultan's feast?" He replied : " In the Presence I did not eat, that advantage might come." The boy rejoined : "Say now your prayers over again, because they had thus no meaning."

Ye who on palm of hand virtues display,
And vice under the armpit hide away,
What look ye—fools and blind—at last
*   to buy*
With such false coin in day of agony ?

VII

I RECALL that in the days of my childhood I was devout, a night - riser for prayers, fond of religion, and abstinent. One night, sitting in the company of my father, I had passed the entire time without once closing my eyes, holding the holy, precious Book to my breast, while many around us were sleeping. So I said to my father : " Among all these not one so much as lifteth his head to perform one act of worship. The sluggards slumber, as though they were dead." To which he answered : "Life of thy father ! if thou didst sleep it would be far better than to be awake, remarking upon the faults of thy fellows."

Self-glory nothing save itself can see,
Before its eyes hangs veil of vanity;
If it had vision, as God hath, not one
Would seem more worthless underneath
  the sun.

VIII

THEY were applauding a certain famous man in an assembly, and speaking of his virtues in exalted language, when he lifted up his face and said : "I am only such as I know myself to be."

Outward, to men's eyes, I go great and
  proud,
Inwardly, for my faults, my head is bowed;
The peacock, praised for beauteous plume
  and pile,
Hates himself for his ugly feet the while.

IX

One of the holy men of Mount Lebanon, whose *makâmât* were famous in all
the western regions, and whose wonderful works were everywhere related, entered the mosque of Damascus, and was
making purification on the brink of the
water of a tank there, when, his foot
slipping, he fell into the reservoir, and
was drawn out of it only with much
pains. When prayers were concluded,
one among those present said : "I have
a difficulty!" The Shaikh asked : "What
is it ?' The worshipper replied : "I call
to mind how once thou didst walk on
the face of the western sea, and thy
sandals were not so much as wetted ;
and to-day from this water, of a man's
stature only in depth, a narrow chance
hath saved thee ! In this what is the
teaching ?" He buried the head of silence in the bosom of meditation, and
then, raising it again, said : "Have ye
not known how Sayed Alum, the Prince
of the World, Muhamad the Chosen One

(on him be the peace and blessing of Allah!), once heard these words: 'There be seasons when thou dost not cease to consort with the angels Jibrael and Michael, and there be seasons when thou art well contented with thy women Hafzeh and Zeynab, because the vision of the Most High discloseth itself and concealeth itself.'"

He showeth now, and hideth now, his face,
That keener be our craving for His grace.

X

IT was once demanded of Yakûb, when he had lost his son, "Oh, glory of our people! Wisest Pîr! Thou didst smell the smell of Yusuf's garment all the way from Egypt, why couldst thou not see him in the pit at Canaan?" Yakûb made answer: "Our condition is the condition of the lightning, one moment all is manifest, one moment all is hidden. Sometimes I sit on the crest of the heavenly dome ; sometimes I cannot see the heels of my own feet."

If always in one state the saint re-mained,
His hands would drop ; Heaven would not be attained.

XI

IN the mosque of Baalbek I was speaking certain sentences of the nature of admonition before an audience whose hearts seemed dead and cold, nor had they ever known the pathway from visible things to those things which are invisible and true. I perceived that the breath of my soul did not reach them ; that the flame of my zeal could not kindle the damp fagots of their spirits. I grew indignant with efforts to instruct such animals, with holding up mirrors in the abode of the blind; but the door of interpretation being still open, the chain of my discourse extended to the explanation of that *ayat*, " We are nearer to him

than his neck-vein," and I was come as
far as saying :

A friend more near than I myself to me,
And yet — most wonderful ! — I cannot
*   see,*
Nor hear, nor know, nor speak one word
*   to Him*
Who yet lives in my blood, bone, vein,
*   and limb.*

I was intoxicated with the wine of
mine own discourse, and the dregs of the
holy cup were at my lips, when a wayfarer passing at the edge of this throng,
caught by the last going - round of that
divine cup, uttered a cry of gladness so
piercing that the whole company par-
took in its ecstasy, and even the most
stupid joined in the rapturous outbreak :
"O God ! those that are far off from
Thee know Thee, and those that are
nighest to Thee are ignorant and sepa-
rate !"

When understanding lacks, no power of
*   speech*
Shall pass into the stubborn soul to teach;

*Widen Desire's plain, the preacher then
Can strike Truth's ball straight to the
     hearts of men.*

XII

ONE night, in the Mecca desert, my
feet, for want of sleep, had not strength
to go farther. I laid my head on the
sand, and bade the camel-driver abstain
from disturbing me.

*The foot-farer shall not go far, me-
     thinks,
When in the dust even the strong camel
     sinks ;
And while fat ones by hunger grow but
     lean,
Lean men may die, no food their lips
     between.*

The camel - man made reply : "Oh,
brother ! Mecca is in front, and robbers* are behind ! If you go on you

* There is a word - play here upon Haram
and Harami.

may live; if you rest here you will
die !"

'Tis sweet to sleep on night of march un-
der the feathery trees,
But wise men know who onward go,
Death cometh soon to these.

XIII

ONCE I saw on the bank of a river a
holy man who suffered from a wound in-
flicted by a tiger, which no medicines
could heal. He had been a long time
afflicted thereby, yet was continually
giving thanks to God, and saying : "Al
hamd' Allah! Glory be to God that I
am stricken by misfortune and not by
sin !"

If the Great Friend assigns to me to die,
Lest ye should deem for love of life I
cry,
Not life I ask, but only this to know :
What unseen sin brings me this right-
eous woe.

XIV

A CERTAIN one, being in hard straits, stole a *gulimî* (a blanket) from the house of a Darweesh, his friend. The Hakim commanded that they should cut off his hand. The owner of the blanket, however, interceded, saying : "I have pardoned him !" "But," quoth the Hakim, "I cannot suffer the line of the law to be set aside on account of an intercession." "Thou hast well spoken," was the reply ; "yet whosoever stealeth from the store of the *wakif*, of property dedicate to religious uses, doth not, by the law, incur mutilation, because that which belongeth to the darweesh is *wakif*, and belongeth already to the poor." The judge upon that withdrew his hand from the prisoner, and said : "Was the world so small that thou couldest only find the abode of such a good one as this to steal from ?" "Ah, Khudâwand!" answered the culprit, "hast not heard what hath been said : ' Ransack the house of a friend at need, but do not so much as knock at the door of an enemy.'"

Give not thy heart to chill despair when evil times begin,
Strip rather from thy foe their coats, and from thy friend his skin.

XV

ONE of the great Sultans said to a holy man, "Cometh recollection of me at any time to thee?" "Yea, lord!" he replied, "whensoever forgetfulness cometh of God!"

Hither and thither goes the man whom God drives from His gate,
But those He calls for guests and friends at no door need to wait.

XVI

A CERTAIN person among the saints saw in a vision of sleep a Sultan sitting in Paradise, and a religious person suffering in Hell, and inquired what was the reason of the elevation of the one

and of the falling downward of the other,
since, said he, " I had myself expected
contrariwise !" They replied : " That
Sultan for his love of pious persons has
ascended to Heaven, and that religious
person, by associating with Sultans, has
gone to Hell."

Thy woollen frock, thy beads, thy rags—
*   what virtue lives in these ?*
Keep thyself clear from inward sin, and
*   wear what thou shalt please !*
No need to ape humility in cap of felted
*   brown ;*
Be Darweesh at thy heart, and then don,
*   if thou wilt, a crown !*

XVII

A WAYFARER with head and feet bare,
coming from Kufeh, joined the Mecca
caravan, accompanying us on the road.
He went swinging along, saying :

No camel do I ride, and no mule - pack
*   do I carry !*
I am not lord of raiyats, nor yet a
*   Sultan's slave !*

My present frets me nothing, and past
troubles did not tarry!
I draw my breath at ease, and I live
the life I have!

One who was mounted upon a camel
cried aloud to him: "Ai, Darweesh!
whither wendest thou? Turn back, or
thou wilt perish of the long road." The
man answered nought, but, with foot on
the desert sand, lightly proceeded.

When we were come to Nakleh-i-Mah-
mood his time arrived for the well-to-do
traveller, and he died. The Darweesh
stood beside his pillow and murmured:
"Here am I alive and well, who had the
hardships; and thou, on thy *bakhti*, thy
fine riding beast, art no more!"

A man there was spent night in tears
beside a sick one's bed;
At dawn the sick one rose refreshed, the
weeping one was dead.
Ah! many a steed of strength and
speed hath foundered on the way,
While some lame jackass limped alive to
closing of the day;

And many an unhurt, healthy one hath
  found his winding-sheet,
While weaklings and sore - stricken men
  live on and drink and eat.

XVIII

A PADISHAH summoned a Darweesh
to his palace. The holy man thought by
taking a medicine to render himself
meagre, so that his Majesty might come
to a better belief of his sanctity, but it
is related that the physic he swallowed
was a poison, and so he died.

He whom, pistachio - nut — all meat, I
  thought,
Peeled like an onion, coat by coat, to nought!
Oh, Darweeshes! with eyes worldward
  alway,
Turn your vile backs to Mecca when ye
  pray!
A Bandah-Khuda art thou? Allah's
  slave?
Well, then, none other master must thou
  have!

XIX

A KAFILAH in the land of Yunan was attacked, and plundered of immeasurable wealth. The merchants set up much grieving and lamentation, calling upon Allah and his Messenger to be their protection, but in vain.

*When the dark-hearted robbers lay hands
   on beast and man,
Little they heed the crying of the scattered caravan.*

Lokman the Wise happened to be with them, and one of the caravan people said to him : "Speak, then, a few words of wisdom and admonition to these robbers, peradventure they may restore to us some little portion of the property, for it would be a pity that all our goods should be lost." The sage Lokman replied : "Say, rather, it would be a pity if words of wisdom should be wasted on such folk !"

*The rusted iron grows not bright, nor
   rugged natures meek;*

Tent-pegs into hard rock to drive only the
foolish seek.

In season of prosperity have hapless ones
in thought,
So shall ye not, for sake of that, to mis-
ery be brought;
Give when the poor man asks of thee,
comfort his falling tears,
Lest what ye saved be torn away by th'
unforgiving years.

XX

FOR all that the Shaikh Shamsuddîn
Abûtfersh Ben Jâsi was wont to say,
bidding me forsake music and counsel-
ling me to lead the quiet life of the
recluse, the spring-time of youth overcame ; and passion and desire prevailing
with me, past restraint, I did frequent
with vast pleasure the company of sing-
ers. At times, when the advice of my
spiritual guide came back to me, I would
recite that verse :

The Kazi, were he in company,
Would clap his hands for pleasure and
glee :
The Mohtasib, quaffing a wine like this,
Would pardon our drunkards their tipsy
bliss.

Until one night I entered the assembly of a sect who had among them a singer—such a singer !

You'd say the string of life must break
with scraping of that bow,
A father howling for dead sons makes
no such sounds of woe.

At times the fingers of my friends were stuffed into their ears, and at times laid sadly on their mouths.

Such singing cannot any please,
Save at the moment when you cease.

When that minstrel broke into voice I said to the master of the house : " For love of God, put quicksilver into mine ear, that I hear him not, or open the door for me that I may flee." Finally, for the sake of my associates, I made submission, and with much self-command sate it through until daybreak.

Too late the Mouzzin called the prayers,
    nor knew
How fast the watches of the darkness
    flew ;
Oh, Mouzzin! take the time from these
    sad eyes,
Which have not closed the night's long
    horror through.

At day dawn, by way of expiation, I took the *dustar* from my head, and some dinars from my girdle, and, placing them before the minstrel, embraced him and gave him many thanks. My friends regarded this conduct as contrary to consistency, and, imputing it to fickleness of judgment, secretly laughed at me; one among them, indeed, lolled out the tongue of ridicule and began to reproach me, saying: "This thy action was not conformable to the conduct of reasonable people —to give the headgear of a holy man to a common singer, and dinars to one who

never before in all his life had a diram
in his hand nor a karat of gilding upon
his drum. Such a performer (God keep
him far from us and this abode of
peace !) is never seen twice in the same
place ! When the uproar proceedeth
from his mouth, the hairs of men stand
on end ! The bird of the balcony in
terror of him flies away. He hath scattered our brains and cracked his own
windpipe." I made reply : "It is well
that thou shouldst quickly draw in the
tongue of complaint, since in my judgment he is one that worketh miracles !"
"Make that thy discovery good," quoth
he, "that we may be in accord, and peradventure ask pardon for the laughter
which hath passed." I answered that
my Shaikh had many a time admon-
ished me as to the duty of avoiding
gatherings for song, with anxious counsels which had not entered an ear of acceptance, until this very night, when a
happy fate and lucky fortune had guided
me to the present place, and to a minstrel through whom I have sworn a vow

never more to be found frequenting
convivial or singing companies.

A soft voice from sweet mouth and rosy
*   lips*
Makes pleasant music, though the art
*   be slight,*
But Ushák, Sifuhán, and Hedjaz* fail
*   From rough throat of a brawler to*
*   delight.*

XXI

THEY put the question to Lokman,
"Where didst thou learn courtliness?"
He made answer, "From those destitute
of good manners, since whatever I observed them do which was unpleasing,
from that I heedfully abstained."

They say not one light word is spoke in jest
*   But the wise man will learning from*
*   it gain;*
Yet to a fool a hundred chapters read
*   Of wisdom, all is jest to him and vain.*

* Musical modes.

XXII

A TALE is told of a religious man who in one night would eat ten *man* of food, and then, before morning, go right through the Namâz from beginning to end. A person of true piety, hearing this, remarked: "It would be far better for him if he had eaten half a loaf, and gone to sleep afterwards."

Keep belly lightly loaded, if mind would
*   wisdom see ;*
For bodies crammed to bursting, make
*   empty souls to be.*

XXIII

THERE was one had forfeited the Heavenly favor by his sins, when suddenly the lamp of Allah's grace, shining upon his road, so gleamed that he was led into the circle of men of true life, and by the felicity of their society, and the blessedness of their spirit, his evil manners became altered into praiseworthy ways, and he withdrew his hands from fleshly things. Yet the tongues of slanderers continued long against him, and they said: "He is still of the former fashion, and his devotion and upright-ness are really not in any earnest."

By tobah—deep repentance—God's anger ye may shun,
But from the bitter tongues of men es-cape in life is none.

Not being able to bear the violence of the tongues which thus reproached him, he carried complaint of it to his spiritual master. The old Shaikh cried for joy, and said : "How canst thou give thanks enough for this blessing, in that thou art so much better than men consider thee to be? Ofttimes wilt thou have to learn how the evil-hearted and envious are on the watch for the faults of the lowly. Yet, if they conspire to shed thy blood, or sit content with wishing ill to thee, rest satisfied with being good, while men speak evil against thee, which is happier than if thou wert bad, while they regarded thee as virtuous. Behold me, of whom all the world cherishes opinions altogether too high, that am nevertheless in the very heart and essence of unworthiness."

Did I live as they will have it, I might
*   be what I would be;*
But we shut the door of selfhood fast
*   and close, that none may see*
Faults and failings. Where's advan-
*   tage? Through all bolts and bars*
*   He spies—*
God, th' All-knowing! hid and open are
*   the same unto His eyes.*

XXIV

I MADE lamentation before a high reputed Shaikh, because a certain one had spread abroad calumnious tales of my misconduct. He replied to me, " Make him ashamed by your rectitude!"

Be yourself good, and let the bad ones rave!
They hold no power to harm save what
*   ye gave.*

If that the strings be all in tune, the lyre
No meddling minstrel's fingers will re-
  quire.

XXV

IT was asked from one of the patriarchs
of Esh-Shams what was the present condition of the sect of Sufîs. He gave
answer : " In times bygone these people
dwelt among men a tribe in outward
appearance miserable, but in reality well-
contented. Now they are a tribe in outward seeming satisfied, but inwardly ill-
content."

When the heart wanders, seeking endless
  change,
And from its own safe solitude doth
  range,
No peace it finds, nor any virtue more ;
But though a man had merchandise in
  store
And rank and wealth and lands, his
  heart being still,
He may live Allah's Darweesh, if he
  will.

XXVI

I HAVE a remembrance how once I had been travelling all night with our caravan, and now towards morning, sleeping at the edge of the desert, I was awakened by an excited person, journeying as our companion on that road, who, uttering a loud cry, and never for a moment ceasing from wild movements, rushed away from us along the sandy path. When it was broad daylight I questioned him, saying : " What was the matter with you ?" He replied, "I heard the bulbuls from the thickets, the red-legged *kabk* from the mountains, and the *gukh*—the frog—from the water, and all the jungle creatures from the desert together uplifting their voices, so I reflected that when the whole creation was thus praising God, each upon his own particular tasbih — his rosary—it could not be becoming that human creatures should lie asleep and voiceless."

*'Twas but a bird at early dawning
 wailed,
Yet over strength, sense, power her note
 prevailed ;
My friend, to whom my cry came, mar-
 velled much
I could be moved to tears and prayers by
 such,
Yea, unto madness ; but I gave reply :
" What! shall a bird praise Allah and
 not I ?"*

XXVII

ONCE I was travelling in the Hedjaz, having for close friends and constant companions some virtuous young men, who at times would break forth into happy singing, and recite divers pleasant verses. An Abid, a devotee, was of our party, and did not like these manners with Darweeshes, of whose secret austerities he was not aware. Presently we arrived at the palm groves of Beni Hallal, where a dark-complexioned boy came forth from an Arab house, and sang to us

with so sweet a voice that the birds flew
down from the air the better to listen.
Even the Abid's own camel, as I observed, started off, dancing to the boy's
music, and, flinging the devotee from his
saddle, ran joyously away into the desert.
"See," I afterwards said, "oh, Shaikh !
the sweet sounds make an impression
on a brute beast, although they can
make none on you !"

*Know'st thou what word the Bulbul sang
    this morning in the grove ?
" What man art thou, that, being Man,
    hast in thy heart no love ?"*

    If a camel will go mad with pleasure
at a desert song, and a man not feel it,
he is but an ass.

*All things make zikr, Allah's praise to
    tell,
The understanding heart knoweth this
    well !
Oh, not alone the Bulbul and the Rose,
But Thorns have tongues to praise Him
    like to those.*

XXVIII

A CERTAIN Sultan, with whom the
course of mortal life was nearly concluded, and who was without an heir,
ordered in his testament that on the
morning following his death, the first
individual entering at the gate of the
city should have the diadem of roy-
alty placed upon his head, and should
be intrusted with the government of
the royal dominions. It befell that the
earliest incomer at the gate after the
Sultan's demise was a *gadâ*, a common
mendicant, who all his life long had
been feeding on scraps, and stitching
rags together to make his clothes. The
ministers—those pillars of the State—
and the nobles—those men of majesty—
duly fulfilled the will of the Sultan, bestowing upon the beggar the kingdom
and the treasury. For a time that Darweesh managed the public affairs well
and ably, until certain among the amir-
ud-dowlats withdrew their necks from
his authority, and the lords of the sur-

rounding countries rose up in contest against him, and prepared their armies. Very soon afterwards his soldiers and people were overborne, and some of his possessions passed from beneath his sway. The royal Darweesh became heart-sore at these events, until one of his old friends, who had been his associate in days of poverty, returning from a tramp, saw him still in an exalted though diminished station, and said: " Praise be to Allah, Lord of all Worthiness and Majesty! inasmuch as high fortune hath helped thee and happy *ikbâl* hath been thy guide—seeing, too, that such a rose hath issued from that old bramble of thine that the thorns have been drawn out of thy foot, and that thou hast attained to such an eminence !"

One bud doth blossom, all the others fall;
One tree gets leaves, the others none at
  all!

The crowned beggar made answer : " Ah, brother! lament for me, since this is no occasion for felicitations ! When thou didst see me last, I had no anxiety except about my next cake of bread. To-day the trouble of all the wide world seemeth to be upon me. If things go amiss I am in distress ; if they go well I am foot-bound in what are called luxuries and pleasures. There is nothing so bad as greatness and state in this world, because if you are prosperous they weary, and if you are unfortunate they overwhelm."

*Wilt thou have wealth ? Seek it in sweet
    content !*
*Envy not him who scatters gold, nor
    praise him !*
*Wise ones have said better than largesse
    spent*
*Is patience for the poor. If Bahram
    braize him*
*A whole wild ass and give't, a locust's
    thigh*
Is to the ant as grand a charity.

XXIX

THERE was one had a friend, busied in the duties of a diwan, and for a long time no occasion had befallen of their meeting. Somebody remarked: " All this while thou hast not seen thy friend." " Nay," answered the other, " and I desire not to see him !" An associate of the diwan was present, who inquired what fault the minister had committed, to make the speaker loath to encounter him. " There is no fault !" said the other ; " but the time for seeing diwans is when they have been disgraced from their dignities. Amid the greatness and splendors of their rule they have no leisure for friendship ; in the day of discomfiture, when they are cast down, they will bring their sorrows back for sympathy."

XXX

ABU HORERU was wont every day to seek the presence of the Chosen One (on him be the blessing and peace of the Most High). On one occasion Muhammad said: "Oh, brother! come not every day, in order that friendship may increase." They said once to a person of learning: "Strange must it seem that though the sun is so splendid and bountiful, we have not heard of any who ever speak of him with love." And the reply came: "It is for the reason that men can see him every day, except in the winter; and then, because he is concealed, he grows longed for."

Frequent your friends! 'tis friendship's
honest proof!
But not so often that they cry, "Enough!"

XXXI

At a time when the society of my friends at Damascus no longer pleased I set my face for the wilderness of El Khuds, and dwelt for a time among the brute beasts. There presently I became a prisoner in the hands of the Franks,

who put me to work in a ditch at Ta-
rabulus, digging clay along with Jews.
But one of the principal men of Aleppo,
with whom I had anciently been friends,
passed that way, and knew me at sight,
and asked : "What condition is this I
find you in, and what are you doing?"
I said :

*To rocks and wastes from man I fled
   away,*
Because, except in God, I found no stay ;
*Judge of my state ! here in a hovel
   chained*
*With men whose evil ways beasts had
   disdained.*
*But better chains, now that a friend I
   see,*
Than a green garden, and such company !

He had compassion on my misery, and
by his moneys freed me from captivity
with the Franks, and, setting me at
liberty, did carry me back with him
to Aleppo. There he had a daughter
whom he gave to me in marriage, to-

gether with a portion of a hundred dinars. But, as time passed, this lady began to display a deplorable character: was quarrelsome, disobedient, and long-tongued, destroying my peace of mind. As has been said:

An evil woman in a good man's home,
It is as if in this life Hell were come!

Beware how thou encounterest such! Once on a certain day, loosening the tongue of reproach, she said: "Art thou not the wretch whom my father bought out of captivity with the Franks for ten dinars?" "Yes," I answered; "for ten dinars he did release me, and for one hundred dinars made me again a captive to thee." As I have heard:

Was one who did by force of arm set
    free,
From claws and fangs of ravening
    wolf, a goat;
But that same evening, all unpiteously,
He put a sharp knife to its bleating
    throat.

125

*"Little I thank thee for!" quoth the
beast, dying.
"From the fierce wolf thou didst deliver me;
Now, vainly on such clemency relying,
I find my worst and fiercest enemy in
thee !"*

XXXII

ONE of the Sultans inquired from a
holy man how he passed the hours of
his pious existence. The saint replied :
"Wellnigh all the night I give to prayers, and in the morning also I would
offer invocations and supplications ; but
the whole day is occupied by close attention to household expenses." Thereupon the Sultan ordered that an allowance should be made for him, sufficient
for daily food, so that the burden of
his family should be taken off his
heart.

*For prisoner bound by homely chains,
No hope of liberty remains !*

Children and debts and clothes and food,
These shut me from all inner good;
By day I think " To-night I'll pray,"
All night I plot to meet the day.

XXXIII

ONE of the devotees of Esh-Shams had
dwelled for many years in the desert,
living mainly on the leaves of trees. The
Sultan of that country paid a visit to
the man, and said : "If it seem to thee,
holy sir ! meet and right, we will pro-
vide a place for thee inside the city,
where thou shalt be in better safety and
happier circumstances of worship than
here, and where others may be benefited
by the spirit of thy pious example, and
imitate thy good deeds." The recluse,
however, did not accept the Sultan's
offer. Then came certain ministers—
pillars of the State—saying, "It would
be fitting, in order to gratify his Majesty, that thou shouldest enter the gates,
and see the nature of this place for a

few days; after which, if the serenity of
thy holy hours be indeed disturbed by
the propinquity of the unblessed, the
choice still remains to thee of departure." And they relate how the devotee
did at length come into the city, and
how the Sultan prepared for him a
palace and garden—a most heart-ravish-
ing and spirit-soothing spot — its scarlet
roses like the cheeks of beautiful damsels,
its hyacinths lustrous as the locks of a
beloved mistress. Even under the sunshine of winter the parterres had the
freshness of a new-born babe that hath
not yet tasted the breasts of the nurse.
The Sultan sent to him, on his arrival
there, a sweet-faced girl:

A countenance fair as the crescent-moon,
deadly to saintly state;
Like an angel's from heaven her beauti-
ful form; her swelling, graceful gait
The pace of the peacock! A sage who
saw, though never so holy and wise,
Were lost to his prayers and his pieties
—finding fresh Paradise.

Furthermore, after her steps followed a slave-boy of the rarest bodily beauty and carriage :

The sight, in seeing him, waxed not content,
As Far-ab * is by water-skins unspent.

This holy man took to daily eating of delicious meats, to the wearing of elegant attire, and also indulged in enjoyment of all sorts of fruits and fragrances, while casting regards upon the handsome slave and lovely damsel — for have not the sages said : " The tresses of beautiful ones are chains upon the feet of prudence, and a snare for the wings of the Bird of Wisdom."

I am the captive Bird, and the Snare
thou ;
For thee heart, faith, and reason are
lost now !

Briefly his worth and dignity in a little space wasted away, after the rule

* The river Euphrates.

which hath been declared that whenever your Vakeel, or your Pîr, or your scholar, or your rhetorician of elevated nature become involved in matters of the flesh they stick fast in their quagmire like a fly's foot in the honey.

The Sultan had, by and by, a desire to see the devotee ; and, paying a visit, found him vastly changed in outward aspect, having a complexion all red and white, and grown to a portly body. He was lapped upon pillows of brocaded silk, and the peri-cheeked girl was standing by his head with a fan of peacock feathers. The Sultan felicitated him on his state of contentment, and conversed with him on many subjects, finishing by the remark : "I have a high regard for two kinds of people in this earth, the learned and the holy." One of the ministers, a man of wisdom, who knew the world, observed: "Oh, my lord, the condition of benevolence stands that towards both tribes of such folks thou shouldest do good. To the learned give gold, in order that others be encouraged to study ; but

to men of religion give nothing if thou
wilt have them continue religious."

Direms and dinars no saint needeth
   much;
When he asks these look somewhere else
   for such!
Who is of holy mind and lives with
   God
Seeks not allowances and pensioned food.

It is as with the beautiful woman un-
adorned :

The finger and the ear-tip show so fair
No turkis and no pearl are needed there.
Yea! he is Darweesh who dwells pure
   and free,
Albeit he eat no bread of charity;
As she is lovely who shows frame and
   face
Which ask no paint, nor gold, nor gems
   to grace.
If, having God, for other goods I faint,
Call me what thing you will—but not
   a saint.

XXXIV

In connection with the foregoing story
this also may be narrated. A Sultan,
being confronted by an important business, declared that if the issue of the
matter fell out according to his desire he
would bestow so many direms among
religious persons. When all had happened according to his wishes, and in
agreement with his promise it was nec-
essary to keep the terms of it, he gave a
bag of direms to one of his trusted servants, bidding him distribute them
among the devotees. The servant, they
report, was prudent and clever. All day
long he wandered round, and at evening
time came back with the direms, which
he laid down before his lord, kissing his
foot, and saying: "I could not find any
Zahids!" "How is that?" quoth his
Majesty. "What tale is this, when I myself know that there are four hundred
in my city?" The servant made answer: "Oh, Lord of the World! Those

who be true Zahids will not receive thy
money, and those who will receive it are
not true Zahids." The Sultan laughed at
this, and said merrily to his surrounding:
"For all that I desired so greatly to benefit these holy men, and had avowed my
desire, this sly-faced fellow sets himself
against me, and, by Allah! hath, moreover, all the right upon his side." For

*When holy men for gold and silver
care,
Search somewhere else for holy men than
there!*

XXXV

FROM one among the very wise and
pious they inquired what he thought
about *nán-i-wakf*, the " bread of pious
purposes." He made reply: "If Darweeshes accept it solely for the sake of
a quiet mind and greater freedom for
devotion, it is lawful, *hallal*. But if they
receive it wholly from an appetite for
food, it is *haram*, unlawful!"

That he may pray the true man takes
thy food,
The false one worships for his belly's
good.

XXXVI

A Darweesh arrived at the abode of a
Saheb of kindly soul. There was a company there around him of pleasant and
witty people, each of whom in turn was
delivering some quip or clever sentiment,
as is the custom sometimes with men of
parts. The Darweesh, who had come
along the desert road, was terribly weary,
and a-hungered beside, not having eaten
anything. One of the company, by way
of a joke, protested that he, too, must
utter something or other. The Darweesh
said: "I have not any wit or elegant imagination like my masters here, nor have
I studied such things, yet there is one
verse with which ye might perhaps put
up just now from me." All of them with
joy and eagerness cried aloud, "*Bigo!*"

(Speak! speak!) whereupon the beggar-
man said :

I'm hungry, and to spy your table's store—
'Tis like a lusty youth of twenty-four
Standing outside the Women's Ham-
mam door.

They were all much amused ; and the
table was ordered anew for him, the lord
of the feast observing: "Oh, friend! wait
a little while, because my people are pre-
paring some *Kuftah* (stewed mince),
which will be delicious!" The Darweesh
lifted his head, and said :

Kuftah upon the table do not lay
Cuffed by the wind and hail; I'll freely
say
*The bread is Kuftah, being on the tray !**

XXXVII

A SCHOLAR said to his master, "What
shall I do, sir, for I am troubled inward-

* There is a Persian pun here.

ly very much by swarms of friends and others who visit me, and my time, which is so valuable, becomes frittered away by their distracting chatter ?" The teacher made reply : " To those who are needy among them advance some small loan, and upon those who are well-to-do make some difficult demand. None of them will hover about you any longer."

If at the head of Islam a beggar marched along,
The Kaffirs would to China fly for terror of his tongue.

XXXVIII

A STUDENT of law said to his father : " None of the eloquent discourses of our doctors affect me at all, because I do not see that a single action on their part corresponds to their words. They preach to men the tark-i-duni (renunciation of the world), but themselves meanwhile eagerly gather up wealth and worldly possessions. The preceptor who merely says, 'Thus and thus do thou,' and stops there, cannot surely influence anybody's heart. A true teacher is he who, knowing sin to be evil, abstains from it, not he who cries to the world, 'Sin not,' and then himself perpetrates evil. Such an instructor—self-indulgent, and pampering his own body — being himself gone astray, how can he give guidance to others?"

The father replied : "Oh, my son ! on the strength of an opinion so usual but so shallow as this of thine, it would be very wrong to turn the face away from the instruction of the competent, and to follow the path of vanity. While accusing the instructed of faults, and while searching for men of wisdom who are immaculate, thou art like to be shut off altogether from the benefits of knowledge ; thus resembling that blind man who, one night, falling into a quagmire, cried aloud, 'Ai, Mussulmanis ! show a lamp that I may see my way !' A woman of the town passing by heard and exclaimed, 'Thou canst not discern a lamp ;

how shalt thou see then by aid of a lamp?' Moreover, the assembly of admonition is like unto the shop of the cloth-seller; until thou hast paid down ready money thou shalt not take any goods away; so there, too, unless thou bringest good inclination thou shalt bear off no happy results." Well was it written :

Hear what by learned men is wisely taught,
With little wisdom though their lives be fraught.
Think not that idle argument goes deep,
"Can he wake others, when himself's asleep?"
Drink wisdom in by eyes, ears—one and all—
Though it be wisdom scrawled upon a wall.

XXXIX

A PERSON of religious life whom I knew quitted the monastery where he had dwelled, and broke the bond of com-

panionship with its devotees to enter a
Madrissa. I asked him: "Between the
society of the religious and the learned
what distinction didst thou perceive
that thou shouldst prefer the college to
the convent?" He answered me:

The Darweesh from the Sea of Sin his
*   own rug strives to save,*
The Hakim drags the souls of men out
*   of that watery grave.*

XL

THERE was a man lying on the high-
road drunken with wine, the bridle of
self-control being slipped from his hand,
when an Abid passed nigh to him, and
cast regards of contempt upon his hateful condition. The young sot lifted up
his head and said:

Thou who art holy, roll not thus thine
*   eyes!*
Nor with such pride a sinful one de-
*   spise!*

139

*Am I so brutish? Better cause that I
Should learn from thee what's real hu-
manity.*

XLI

A TAYIFA of reprobates got into dis-
putation with a student of religion, and
by uttering evil words hugely distressed
him. He carried his complaint to the
ears of his Pîr, telling what had befallen. That personage said : " Ah, son !
the *Khirka* of a Darweesh is the garment
of resignation. Whoever wearing such
a dress cannot bear evil-speaking and
contumely is an enemy to his faith, and
those holy rags misbecome him."

*A great stream grows not muddy by
one stone,
A Darweesh vexed is like a puddle blown;
If wrong be done, thine injurers forgive,
By pardoning them thyself may'st par-
doned live !
Ah, brothers ! since the last day brings
to dust,
Be dust and ashes now, as then we must.*

XLII

HEAR now this little story: Once in Baghdad a contention fell out between the Flag and the Purdah. The Flag, by reason of the dust of the road and the worry of the staff-leather, said, in a temper of high displeasure, to the Curtain: "Thou and I be both servants of one master, slaves in the court of the same Sultan; but I never for one moment obtain respite from duty, being continually upon the march. Thou, on the contrary, dost experience no kind of trouble. Thou art not called upon to storm the walls of the Hissar, or to traverse the desert, or confront the storm - ring (whirlwind) and the sand. In every adventure my foot goeth first; why, therefore, is thy glory greater than mine? Thou dwellest amid moon-faced slaves and damsels scented with jasmine; I am roughly borne by men-at-arms, my feet tied in the flag-stirrup, my head ruffling in the breeze." Meekly replied the Purdah: "I lay my head

141

upon the threshold ; thou liftest up thine own to the sky. Whoso stretcheth forth his neck too far exposes himself to neck-wringing."

XLIII

ONE of the Lords of Wisdom observed a public wrestler mightily enraged and foaming at the mouth. Inquiring what was the matter, some one explained that the man had been the subject of some abuse. The sage remarked : "This ridiculous person can lift a thousand *man* of rock, but cannot support the weight of one single evil word."

Pride in brute strength and noisy beasts
resign,
Man while you fight, and woman when
you whine :
Make sweet the mouths of men by decent
deed,
'Tis better than to bash them till they
bleed ;

If one could tear the trunks from ele-
phants,
He is not man who human feeling wants:
Since Adam's sons are moulded from
the clay,
'Tis only mortal to be humble—pray!

XLIV

THEY questioned a distinguished person among the Sûfis as to the way of
life among that brotherhood. He replied : " The least among their merits is
that their passion for the good of their
fellows is greater with them than care
for their own affairs ; and the wise have
laid it down, ' No brother is he, nor so
much as even a kinsman, who is brother
and kinsman only to himself.' "

Who goes the road with us must keep beside,
No fellow traveller if he outstride.
Bind not thy heart to one who will not be
Heart-bound. Of blood-relations e'en live
free
Where there is kinship but not piety!

143

I call to mind how a certain opponent
did take umbrage at the thought in this
verse, alleging that in the Glorious Book
the Most High Allah hath prohibited the
abandonment of connection with rela-
tives, commanding us to rather esteem
friendship with them beyond that with
any others, so that what I had cited was
contrary to the Sacred Word. But I
made answer that he was wrong, and
that my verse was conformable to the
Koran. Allah hath said: "If a man's
parents bid him to join any as partners
with me, let him not obey them." Also,
it is written :

From fifty score of kinsfolk far better
shalt thou part
Than one true-spoken stranger with the
fear of God at heart.

XLV

A MAN of law possessed a daughter of
extreme ugliness, for whom, when arrived at the marriageable age, he could

find no willing suitor, albeit a good dower and possessions besides were attached to her person.

If she who wears them doth ill-favored show,
Lustrous brocades and silks lose half their glow.

In fine, by the behest of necessity, he tied her nuptial knot with a blind man. About the same time, the story runs, there arrived from Sûndeya a famous Hakim, who could restore vision to the sightless. They inquired from the man-of-law why he did not apply the treatment to his son-in-law. " Nay, nay !" says he ; " I fear if he became clear-sighted he might divorce my daughter."

The husband of the ugly wife
Is better blinded all his life.

XLVI

THERE was a Sultan who turned a special eye of contempt upon all the

tayifas of the Darweeshes. One among
these, quick at perception, discovered
his Majesty's sentiment, and said : " Oh,
Malek, we, in this world, are far below
thee now, as regards station and state,
but in love of our kind much happier.
In death all shall be equal, and on the
Judgment Day we shall be thy supe-
riors."

The lord of many lands hath all wants
  fed,
The Darweesh ofttimes lacks a crust of
  bread;
Yet both at hour of death will bear
  away
Only a winding-sheet to house of clay;
Ah! at that time, for beggar and for
  king,
Light loads pack easiest for far journey-
  ing.

In outward garb the Darweesh goes
ragged and with a shaven pate, but the
truth dwells living in his heart, and his
sensual self hath been vanquished.

CONCERNING DARWEESHES

He waiteth not at Accusation's door,
And being injured injureth none the
more ;
If from the Hill of Fate a rock roll
down,
The man of faith sits where he sate
before.

The rules of the true recluse are *zikr*,
commendation; and *shukur*, thankful-
ness ; and *khidmut*, serviceableness; and
tá'at, obedience ; and *aithar*, almsgiving;
and *kaná'at*, contentment ; and *towahéd*,
profession of unity ; and *tavakkul*, reli-
ance ; and *tasalidn*, rendering obedience ; and *tahammul*, endurance. Whoever is endued with these qualities is
a Darweesh indeed, though he wear a
splendid dress ; but one who utters fool-
ishness, one who lives without prayer ;
a worshipper of his own desires, a sen-
sualist ; one who turns night into day in
the bonds of concupiscence, and day into
night with the sleeps of sloth ; one who
eats and drinks all he can, and speaks
whatever cometh to his tongue — he is

Rand, a profligate, even though he wears the *dalak* of a Darweesh.

Oh thou that hast of holiness the seem-
  ing outward dress,
With inside void of piety, and filled with
  rottenness!
Hang not a curtain, Hypocrite! of many
  colored sheen
At door of that low reed-hut where thy
  vile soul lives unseen!

XLVII

I saw some fresh-blown roses, a great handful of them, tied upon a gateway with some grass, and I asked, "What is grass — mere common grass — that it should thus dwell in the company of roses?" The grass spake full sorrowfully : "Khamoosh, keep silence! The kind-minded forget not their associates! Albeit I possess neither beauty, nor rich color, nor fragrance, yet am I a herb of the Garden of God; I also am a servant among the servants of the Hasrat, the

Eternal Presence, by whose bounty I have been nourished until now, so that whether I be destitute of all dignity, or whether by His grace I possess any merit, in my Lord is my trust and my desire. Notwithstanding that I have no ability to serve Him, and no methods of my own for obedience, He is able to employ the willingness of his humble slave, who hath himself no strength or virtue. It is the custom, moreover, that the lords of contract should set free their bondsmen when they are old."

Oh, Sadi! take the Temple road, the
way of humbleness,
Oh, Man of God! walk in the path
which goes with gentilesse!
Ill falls the foot that wanders! that
stumbles in its pride:
This is the gate to Righteousness, there
openeth none beside!

XLVIII

THEY inquired of a Hakim which was the greater, Courage or Liberality? His answer was, "Whoso practiseth liberality hath not need of courage. It is written on the tomb of Bahram - Goor : ' The hand of bounty is better than the arm of Strength.' "

Dead long ago is Hatim Tai, yet his
name lives brightly on
For noble works of largesse and deeds
of bounty done ;
Give of thy store! the vine-dresser lops
many a branch away
That grapes may hang the thicker at
time of harvest-day !

THE GULISTAN

OR

ROSE-GARDEN

OF

SHAIKH SA'DI

Gateway the Third

THE EXCELLENCY OF MODERATION

THE EXCELLENCY OF MODERA-
TION

I

A NEGRO mendicant from the West, walking through the quarter of the cloth-merchants of Aleppo, was heard to say: "Ai, lords of much riches! if ye, so wealthy, knew justice, and we, so poor, possessed contentment, my trade of begging would be at an end."

Oh, fair Contentment! make me rich
  with thee!
For wealth, lacking such gift, is pov-
  erty;
To nook of patience Lokman happy went,
For none is wise who is not patient.

II

THERE were two Amir-zadahs, sons of a great man in Egypt, of whom one attained great learning, the other immense possessions, so that the former grew to be the wisest personage of his time, while the latter became Aziz-i-Misr, the Lord of Egypt. In later days the wealthy Prince cast the eye of contempt upon the erudite one, his brother, and said: "I have arrived at the Sultanate, whilst thou abidest in thy old penury as at first." The poor man answered: "Oh, my brother! needs must I thank the most High God for His favor in this, that I have acquired the heritage of the Prophets, that is to say, Wisdom; while thou hast only reached to the inheritance of Fara'un and of Hâmân—namely, the throne of Egypt."

I am the ant who underfoot doth go,
And not the wasp men curse for sting-
   ing so;

*How shall I not laud Allah loud and
    long,
Who hath bereaved me of the power to
    wrong?*

III

I HEARD about a Darweesh who was
burning slowly on the fire of poverty,
and stitching patch after patch upon his
old rags, but who found consolation in
this *bai't* which he would hum :

*Gladly I munch my hunk of bread, and
    wear the rags you see,
Because to be beholden is worse than
    starving free.*

Somebody said to him, "Wherefore
dost thou remain thus, when there is
many a one in the city of most kindly
nature who possesses bowels of noble
compassion towards religious folk in distress, ever sitting at the doors of suffering hearts. On growing acquainted with
thy condition, such a man would hold
it his duty to succor the necessities of

one of God's favorites." " Khamoosh !" answered that devotee, " be silent ! for to perish of want is better than to carry our woes before people;" and wise ones have said :

Sit in the corner of Content! patches
  on patches stitch!
'Tis happier than to cadge for clothes,
  petitioning the rich;
By God! 'twere less the pains of Hell
  with good resolve to meet,
Than to be spurned to Paradise by un-
  concerning feet.

IV

ONE of the monarchs of Persia despatched a physician of high skill to take service with Mustapha (may peace be upon him !). He remained some years in Arabia, without anybody coming to him, even for consultation, and no one asked him even once for physic. One day, standing in presence of the Chief of all Prophets (peace be ever with him !),

the physician complained of this, saying :
" They did send me hither for the purpose of furnishing medicines to thy
friends and followers; yet all this while
not a soul hath made recourse to me, so
that thy servant might discharge the
task laid upon him." The holy Rasul
(may the peace of Allah remain with
him!), replying, said : "It is the habit
with my people never to eat a mouthful
until the call of hunger demands, and to
abstain from food while something of
appetite still remaineth." The physician
bowed, and spake : "Truly that is the
way to preserve a perfect health," and
therewith he departed, having first kissed
the dust of obedience.

The doctor waves his hand or nods his
  head
Only when something fitting must be said;
When too free food the pampered body
  fills,
Or too long fasting bringeth weakly ills,
Then may he safely counsel that thy board
Not too much nor too little shall afford.

V

One who made many oaths of amend-
ment and afterwards brake them, was
thus addressed by an old Shaikh : "I
know that thou hast the habit of glutton-
ous feeding, and that thou dost seek to
restrain thine appetites, which would
burst an iron chain, with the cord of thy
good resolutions, which is thinner than a
hair. Beware, for the day will arrive
when they will destroy thee !"

*He who a wolf-cub kept, the beast to
tame,
Was torn to pieces when to wolf it came.*

VI

In the *Sîrst* of Ardashîr Bâbukan it
stands related how he inquired from a
physician of Arabia what amount of food
ought to be consumed in a single day.
The Hakim said that the weight of a

hundred direms should suffice. Ardashîr asked how life could be sustained on so limited a quantity, and the physician replied: "It is enough to keep you alive, and in regard of what thou eatest beyond this thy belly is the mere hamal of thy meat."

Food is for life, and therewith praise to
*   Heaven ;*
Life's not for food, nor mouth for guz-
*   zling given !*

VII

Two Darweeshes of Khorasân had formed a close companionship, and were travelling together. One, being weakly, ate only every second night, and the other, being robust, would take food three times a day. It befell that at the gate of a city they came under suspicion of being spies, and were both flung into the same cell, the door of it being plastered up with mud. After two weeks it was found that they were guiltless, and

the door was opened. The strong man
was lying dead, but the weak one had
carried his life safe through the trial.
The city people were amazed, but a
Hakim remarked that the contrary
would rather be wonderful, because the
constant eater had no habit or faculty
of abstinence, while the other one, holding his body under control, and inured
to patience, more easily endured.

VIII

A HAKIM there was who warned his
son against overeating, because gluttony
causes illness. The boy said : " Oh, father, hunger slayeth; and hast thou not
heard what hath been told by the wise
that it is better to die of a surfeit than
to put up with hunger ?" The father
responded : " Nevertheless, have thou
regard to moderation !"

*Eat not so much that ye be choked like
    swine,*
Eat not so little that your bodies pine.

Food is to nurture life — but, too much
  meat !
'Twere better you should bitter poison
  eat.
Gulashkar—rose-cakes—irk the over-fed,
But hungry stomachs love the driest
  bread.

IX

THEY questioned a sick man what in
his heart he most wished for. His answer
was : "I most of all desire not to desire
anything !"

When belly with bad pains doth swell,
It matters nought what else goes well.

X

A FLESHER there was in the city of
Wasit who had dealings with the Sufis
to the extent of some direms, and did
ask for payment every day with much
violence of speech. The association, by
reason of his reproaches, had sore livers ;
but there was no help except by pa-

tience. A worthy man among their number sorrowfully observed : " Ye can more easily put off appetite by promise of food than this butcher with promise of money !"

Better forego the rich man's aid
Than at his gate to cower afraid ;
Better for lack of collops die
Than face such importunity.

XI

A CERTAIN brave man, in battle with the Târtars, received a dreadful wound. Some one remarked to him that there was a merchant who possessed a sovereign electuary for hurts, and might give him some if requested. But that same merchant was infamous for his niggardliness.

If on his board, in lieu of bread, there
*   lay the golden sun,*
No man had shared his sunshine till
*   day of judgment—none !*

The brave man made reply : " If I shall ask for the medicine, he may give it, or he may not give it ; and if he give it, it may do me good, or not do me good ; so that in any case it is all much the same as deadly poison. Whatever one obtains from grudging givers by entreaty may help the body but must damage the soul, and wise ones have declared that if the Ab-i-hayat (the Water of Immortality) were to be had at the price of honor, the good man would not buy it, because to die with credit is better than to live with disgrace."

From a kind hand the colocynth tastes sweet,
And sweetmeats bitter when a churl bids eat.

XII

ONE among the learned, who had many mouths to fill at home, and but scanty means, told his plight to a great personage with whom he had formerly stood

in high estimation. The great man re-
sented the application, as not becoming
any personage of self-respect, and made
an evil face over it.

When ill-luck sours thy visage do not wend,
Taking thy sick looks to a cherished
friend;
For thou dost spoil his pleasure by thy
woe;
But with a countenance of courage go,
Pleasant and bold—so shall the matter
speed,
And, with an open brow, he'll meet thy
need.

They relate that, in respect to the woe-
begone one's *wasif*, the great man something augmented it, but the warmth of
his good-will suffered diminution. After
some days the petitioner himself remarked this failure of the old feeling
and mournfully observed :

He made my loaf large, but mine honor
small;
Than agony of asking best lack all!

XIII

A HOLY man being in straits, somebody said to him : " There is such an one who hath wealth beyond counting. If he were made acquainted with thy necessity, he would permit no delay in readjusting that." The Darweesh responded : " But I know him not !" Quoth the other: "I shall perform the service of conducting you thither," and so took him by the hand, until they reached the abode of the rich man. There the Darweesh saw one sitting gloomily with a hanging lip, and without a word turned round again and came back. " What didst thou with him ?" inquired his friend. " Why," says the holy man, "he gave me the pleasure of a sight of him, and I made him a present of his bounty !"

Carry no suings to the crabbèd-faced,
Where hard glance sends thee back
ashamed, disgraced ;
If thou must bare thy heartache, let it be
To one whose smile speaks ready sympathy.

XIV

A year of drought befell in Iskandersh, of such severity that the restraints of human patience were relaxed—the doors of heaven seeming to be shut against the supplications of the people, which vainly ascended to them.

No creature was there of the earth, or
sky,
Or water—all that creep, and swim, and
fly—
But sent up lamentations, lacking food.
'Twas strange that rcek of sorrow did
not brood
Into a tear-cloud under the fierce sun,
And fall in deluge o'er the land undone.

In that same year there was in the city a mûkhannas—an hermaphrodite—(God keep us from the like !) whom to descant upon would be the abandonment of politeness, particularly in the hearing of superior people, while on the other hand, lest it be set down by some to the incompetence of the present narrator, he must not wholly pass over the description of the man, and will here, therefore, for brevity, cite but two verses, by way of hint and guidance, since from one word many may be gathered, and ye shall judge of a whole ass's load by a single handful.

If any Tatar slew him where he stood,
No righteous judge would ask the Tatar's blood:
Thou Bridge of Baghdad! how long wilt thou go,
Men on the top of thee, water below?

The personage, then, of whose habits a partial glance hath been so afforded, possessed wealth beyond imagination, and lavished gold and silver upon the empty-handed, providing also a well-spread table for travellers. A band of Darweeshes, who by pinch of famine had come to the point of life or death, took thought to share his bounty, and asked counsel from me. I drew my head back from consenting. I repeated to them this verse :

The lion a hound's leavings will not eat,
Though in his den he die for lack of
meat.

Rather yield up your bodies to the
helplessness of hunger than hold forth
beseeching hands to the worthless.

Count not the vile thy friends, albeit
they be
Prouder than Feridûn, and rich as he;
When knaves their muslins and brocades
display,
'Tis gold and lazuli on mounds of clay.

XV

THEY asked of Hakim Tai: "Hast
thou seen, or hast thou heard of one in
all the world more remarkable than thyself for greatness of mind?" "Yea!" he
replied; "on a certain day I did slaughter
forty camels for a feast, and afterwards,
riding with an Arab Omrah on the edge
of the desert, I saw a hedger and ditcher
who had collected a fagot of thorns.

'Why goest thou not, oh friend,' I said, 'to the feast of Hakim Tai, since throngs of folk are flocking to his victuals?'" He answered me :

He who by sweat of brow's his own bread-winner
Should owe no thanks to Hakim for a dinner.

I regarded that person, for great-mindedness and manhood, as very much my superior.

XVI

MOOSA the Prophet (may the peace of Allah be upon him!) saw a Darweesh who, by reason of his nakedness, had covered his body up with sand. The man cried : "Ya, Moosa ! say a prayer for me to God that He may send me clothing and subsistence, since by want of strength I am dwindling to a ghost!" So Moosa (on whom be peace!) made supplication, and God sent the man subsistence. Some days subsequently, when

169

the prophet was coming from devotions,
he saw the Darweesh a prisoner, with a
crowd gathered around him, and inquired: "What hath happened with
this one?" The people said: "He hath
drunk wine, and engaged in a conflict
whereby he killed a man, and now we
are executing the law upon him."

If prowling cats had wings as they have
legs,
They would not leave us any sparrows'
eggs;
And when a base man comes to power
and pelf,
He twists the wrists of weaker than
himself.

Moosa (on whom be the peace of Allah !) confessed the wisdom of the Crea-
tor, and begged forgiveness for his own
presumption, uttering an Ayat from the
Koran.

When churls win dignities and things of
cost,
A clout upon their skulls is wanted most.

EXCELLENCY OF MODERATION

This is most certain!   Wise was he who
*   sings,*
"'Twere better if the ant never had
*   wings."*

A father may have honey in plenty,
but will not give it to a son who is burning with fever.   Verily, He who hath
not made thee rich knew what was well
for thee better than thyself.

XVII

I saw an Arab sitting in a ring of
jewel-dealers at Basra, and telling a
story how once upon a time in the
desert he had lost his road, and had not
a morsel of food remaining, so that he
had settled in his heart that he must
die. "Suddenly," said he, "I lighted
upon a bag which felt to be full of grain.
Never can I forget the zûk wa shâdi—
the relish and the joy—of thinking that
it was indeed parched corn, and then
again the agony and despair to find it
was only a bag of pearls.

The desert traveller mid the driving
sands,
Sinking with thirst—what matter if his
hands
Hold pearls or dust? His dried mouth
curseth both!
So, when a man with hunger falls to die,
What difference whether in his girdle-
cloth
He hideth gold or only frippery?

XVIII

THERE was, indeed, an Arab traveller
who became lost in the great wilderness. His provisions, and with them his
strength, all gave out, and only some
direms were left in his waistband. Long
he wandered without finding the path,
and at last perished in his misery. A
company of men afterwards passed that
way and saw the direms scattered in
front of his head, and there were written
with finger-point on the sands these
words:

Lie there, thou gold! What's all earth's
gold
To him that must not live?
For one boiled turnip all my gold
And silver I would give.

XIX

NEVER did I complain of the chances
of fortune, nor make a wry face at the
resolution of fate, but once, when I was
brought to the pass of going barefoot-
ed, and had nothing with which to buy
shoes. Just then I entered the mosque
at Kusa with a heavy heart, and there I
observed a person who had no feet at
all. At this I offered up praise and
thanks to the Almighty God, and gladly submitted to this accident of being
shoeless.

To one well fed a roasted chicken means
Less than a plate of common kitchen
greens;
But unto him that hath no food to eat,
A cabbage, like a roasted fowl, seems sweet.

XX

A SULTAN there was who, being gone
a-hunting with some few of his attendants, in the winter, got belated towards
nightfall in a spot far from any inhabit-
ed place. They came upon the hut of a
rustic, and the Sultan said : "We will
make refuge here, to escape the pinch
of cold." One of the Wuzeers objected
that it would ill befit the dignity of a
prince to seek shelter in the abode of a
common peasant, and said it would be
better to pitch a tent and kindle a fire.
The peasant, informed of the Sultan's
arrival, hastily prepared from his scanty
store what food could be easily cooked,
and, taking it to the Sultan, kissed the
dust of obeisance, and spake : "The
lofty glory of my lord can suffer no
lessening by condescending to his slave,
but these fine people did not wish that
a poor man should have honor." His
speech pleased the Sultan, who accordingly spent the night in his cottage, and
at morning-time bestowed upon him

money and a *khilât* of honor. I further heard how the peasant walked a few steps at the stirrup of the Prince, and uttered this :

From my lord's greatness and high maj-
esty
Nought is abated that he lodged with
me,
But higher than the sun has risen my
head
Since o'er it such a gracious shade was
spread.

XXI

THERE is a story of a disagreeable fellow who had amassed much wealth, and one of the Sultans made application to him, saying : "It appeareth that thou dost possess boundless riches, and as we have an important business to settle, if thou wilt advance us a little of this, in way of loan, when our revenues come in it shall be returned." The man replied: "It doth not become the dignity of a Lord of the World, such as thou art, to

175

foul the palm of magnanimity with the
money of a *gadá'i* like me, collected scrap
by scrap." The Sultan answered : " Irk
thyself not on that account, for we shall
bestow it on the Tatars !"

*Though water from a Christian well's
 unfit,*
*What odds, when a dead Jew we wash
 with it?*

I heard that he turned his head away
from the Sultan's request, and com-
menced to haggle and make insolent
eyes. On that his Highness commanded the cause of his misbehavior to be
taken from him by violent methods :

When by fair means no gains betide,
*Needs must that foul means should be
 tried;*
Who doth not of a good grace give,
Will see kings take without his leave.

XXII

I MET a merchant who owned one hundred and forty camels and fifty slaves

and porters. One evening, on Kish Island, he took me to his lodging, and did not cease all the night through from foolish talk like this: "Such and such of my property lies in Turkestan; and such and such goods are in Hindustan; and this document is the contract for such and such an estate, and such an one is my security." Then would he go on: "I have sometimes the desire to wend to Iskanderieh, where the climate is good; and sometimes I say 'No,' because the sea of the West is stormy. Oh, Sa'di! there is yet only one long journey before me, and, that accomplished, I will sit in my own little corner and give up business." I inquired what journey that was to be. He answered me: "I want to carry sulphur of Persia to China, which in that country, as I hear, bears a high price; and thence to take Chinese ware to Roum; and from Roum to load up with brocades for Hind; and so to trade Indian steel—*púlad*—to Halib. From Halib I will convey its glass to Yemen, and carry the painted cloths of Yemen back

M   177

to Persia. Afterwards I will give up
trade, and take mine ease in my shop."
So much of such nonsense he poured
forth as at last to be unable to chatter more, and then said : "Thou, too,
oh Sa'di! tell me something about the
things which thou hast seen and heard."
Whereat I rejoined :

A lord there was set forth to cross the
wilderness of Ghor,
He tumbled from his camel, and he
never travelled more;
Ah, greedy eyes of those that toil, roving
from spot to spot,
'Tis grave-dust that must fill ye, if con-
tentment fills ye not.

XXIII

I HEARD tell of a rich person who was
as famous for niggardliness as Hakim
Tai for liberality. In outward appearance he showed magnificent, but the
meanness of his soul was such, and so
essential to his nature, and so rooted,

that he never gave so much as a crust
of bread to anybody, and would not have
pelted with one morsel the cat of Abu
Horeiru, nor flung a bone to the dog of
the Companions of the Caves. In effect
no man ever saw his door open or his
table spread. The passing beggar tasted
no more of his victuals than he could
win by smell, and of his bread-breakings
the birds got never a crumb. It was related to me how, upon the Sea of the
West, voyaging to Egypt, with all the
pride of a Pharaoh in his head, suddenly
an adverse wind beat upon his ship, and
a tempest arose. He lifted up hands of
supplication and began to make useless
prayers.

What profits "God be pitiful" and
*   hands in danger raised*
To him who in prosperity not once said,
*   " God be praised?"*
Buy with thy white and yellow good
*   for others,*
It shall bring weal to thee as to thy
*   brothers.*

This is a house will last when thou art
dead,
With bricks of gold and silver 'stab-
lishèd.

Some poor relations in Egypt inherited
his possessions and became rich thereby.
They tore up their old clothes at his
death, and fashioned themselves new
ones from silks and brocades. That
very week I saw one of them riding a
steed, fleet-footed as the wind, and a
fair-faced gholam running behind him,
whereupon I said to myself :

Wah ! if the dead should come to life
again
Amidst his wives and kinsmen, would
the pain
Of all this gear relinquished not be
keener
Than even their sorrow when they knew
him slain ?

By reason of an old friendship existing
between us I pulled the sleeve of that
rider, and said :

EXCELLENCY OF MODERATION

Eat and enjoy, oh worthy one! the goods
thy luck did send
From him of Destiny deject, who saved
but would not spend.

XXIV

THERE happened a stout fish into the
net of a feeble old fisherman, who had
not strength enough to secure it, so that
the fish got the better of its captor, and
went away, taking the net with it. What
saith the verse?

The slave went to the river to fill his
water-jar;
He brought none, for the river rose and
washed his corpse afar.

Every other time the net had taken
the fish; this time the fish departed,
taking away the net. The other fishermen were vexed, and vented reproaches
against their companion for having en-
closed such a prey and not being able to
bring it ashore. He said: "Ah, my

brothers! what could I do? seeing it was not my day for luck, while the fish had yet more of existence destined to him?"

Bereft of luck, the fisherman in Tigris
  catcheth naught;
And, not yet doomed, the fish that kicks
  upon the sand's uncaught.

XXV

THERE was a man who, having neither hands nor feet, killed an insect of the kind called "thousand-legs." A pious person passing by exclaimed: "*So-bahn Allah!* Holy God! For all the thousand limbs that this creature possessed, here is one comes along with no arms and no legs and the beast doth not escape from him!"

When the soul-seizer comes behind, he
  stays the fleetest foot;
Death's breath once felt on warrior's
  neck, vain is it if he shoot.

EXCELLENCY OF MODERATION

XXVI

I saw once a foolish fellow, very fat, his body clad in a costly robe of honor, riding on a high - bred horse, and with muslin of Egypt wound round his head for a turban. Somebody said to me: "Oh, Sa'di! How regardest thou this rich brocade wrapped upon a creature so ignorant?" I replied: "He remindeth me of ill writing done in golden ink."

Naught unto men resembleth in this ape,
Except his coat and hat and outward
*   shape.*
Nothing is his of all this gear and
*   good,*
Wealth, worldly show, save his vile,
*   muddy blood!*
Think not, if one fall poor, of noble
*   mind,*
His dignity thereby must be declined;
Nor deem a rich knave noble, tho' he
*   thrives,*
And gold nails in his silver threshold
*   drives.*

XXVII

QUOTH a thief to a beggar : " Hast
thou not shame to hold thy hand forth
in front of every stingy fellow who
passes for a mite of money?" The mendicant answered :

*Two barleycorns of silver are better in
    the hand
Than for a dang and half a dang to
    have it shorn by brand.*

XXVIII

THEY relate the story of a young
athlete who, by contrarieties of fortune,
had come to the question of life or death,
and with craving belly and empty hands
repaired to his father, and requested in-
dulgence for his desire for travel, urging
that by the strength of his arms he
might perhaps lay hold of the hem of
Fortune's garment :

EXCELLENCY OF MODERATION

Good gifts and skill are vain, until dis-
cerned,
Musk must be rubbed and aloes* must
be burned.

The father said : " Ah, my son ! thrust forth absurd imaginations from thy head, and draw the foot of discontent back into the skirt of safety, since the wise ones have declared that wealth accrueth not by endeavor so quickly as the lust of it may be overcome."

No man by tricks can Fortune's skirt
surprise,
Nor with collyrium cure a blind man's
eyes.
If for each hair thou hadst two hun-
dred gifts,
They would not steel thee 'gainst ill fort-
une's shifts.
What can the strong, but luckless, hope
to catch ?
Thine arm 'gainst Fate's finds an une-
qual match.

* Lignum aloes.

The son said: "Oh, my father! of journeying the benefits are many, *videlicet*, the freshness it bringeth to the heart, the profitable acquisitions, the seeing and hearing of marvellous things, the delight of beholding new cities, the coming into contact with unknown friends, the obtaining of reputation, the learning of high manners, the augmentation, maybe, of goods, the experiences as to livelihood, novel connections, and familiarity with the world; for which reasons the guides of the *Tarífat*—those Masters of the Path of Life—have declared:

While thou dost cleave to house and shop
thou art but half a man!
Go, see the great world for thyself, whilst
Destiny cries 'Can.' "

The father made reply: "Oh, my son! the excellences of travel, as thou hast named them, are assuredly numerous, but these are reserved for five descriptions of mankind. First, there is the merchant, who, being one of large means and influence, hath slaves, and heart-entangling handmaids, and sharp serving-men, wherewith he may every day visit a new city, and every night sleep in a different place, enjoying all the luxuries of the world.

He that owns wealth, in mountain, wold,
    and waste,
Plays master — pitches tent at his own
    taste ;
Whilst he who lacks that which the world
    commands
Must pace a stranger, e'en in his own
    lands.

"Secondly, there is the learned person, who, by sweet persuasiveness and the power of speech, and his gathered wisdom, causes people, wherever he goeth, to show him deference and treat him with attention.

A wise man's presence is like gold re-
    fined,
Everywhere money and its value
    known ;

Fools are those counters no folks will be blind
To take for current coin except their own.

" Thirdly, there is the person of handsome bearing, towards whom the inner selves of people turn, desiring his companionship, and deriving from it great pleasure, and considering service to such a distinction. Accordant to what hath been said : ' Good looks are better than great riches. A sweet face is balm to sore hearts, and the key to closed doors.'

Fair faces will win favor south and north,
Though father and though mother drive them forth ;
There was a peacock's feather in The Book
Laid 'mid those holy leaves. ' An honor took
Insultingly !' I cried. But the plume said,
' Silence, good friend, since unto goodlihead

EXCELLENCY OF MODERATION

And grace is everywhere right proper
  room,
And all with joy receive us where we
  come.'

When in the child beauty and charm
  reside,
None asks the father's name, nor aught
  beside :
' A pearl it is,' they cry, 'inside its shell !
Let it not stop ! Such is to buy and
  sell !'

"Fourthly, should travel a sweet-voiced
one, who with a throat like David's stops
the very stream in its course, and stays
the birds in the air ; much more by the
aid of such accomplishments may he
take the hearts of men prisoner, and
cause even the wise to display pleasure
in his society."

How ravishing to lovers' ears, with wine
  of morning mad,
At dawn of day some tender lay, sung
  musical and sad ;

*Ah! better than a handsome face I deem
a lovely voice,
For that brings pleasure to the sense;
this makes the soul rejoice.*

"Fifthly, the artificer should travel, he who by skill of fingers can obtain livelihood, so as to keep his self-respect from the dishonor of asking for bread. This accords with the saying of the wise:

*Cobbler or patcher — if they quit their
home—
No want or woe fear, wheresoe'er they
roam;
But if the Sultan of Nimráz should creep
Forth from his kingdom he would hungry sleep.*"

These five qualifications, then, said the father, as described, are those which upon a journey bring peace to the spirit, and are the causes of satisfaction. But whoever is destitute of all of them will go forth into the world with vain expectations, and nobody will hear of his name or purpose.

EXCELLENCY OF MODERATION

On this revolving wheel of earthly state
Whoso is ear - marked by the hand of
Fate
Goes falsely tempted; like the foolish
dove
Which—destined not to see his nest and
love—
Flies by the way that brings to grain
and trap,
And, self-misguided, makes his own mis-
hap.

Quoth the son : "But how, oh my
father ! shall I fly in the face of that
maxim of the prudent who say : ' Albeit
the daily elements of life are apportioned
for all, yet it is indispensable to have recourse to the means for obtaining them ;
and although mishap be foreordained,
it is still proper to avoid the gateways
by which it may enter '?

Cometh, no doubt, our daily food, yet way
of sense is so
That we should seek it from outside, and
where it groweth go ;

And we must die at time of death, yet
no man holds it law
For that, to run, ere life be done, into
the dragon's jaw.

"In my present condition I am strong
enough to fight with a furious elephant,
or to wrestle to the ground a ravening
lion ; and it is all the fitter that I should
journey, because my spirit will not endure poverty.

When a man falls from dignity and
grace,
Why eat more dirt ? The whole world
is his place !
Each night the rich one for his serai
makes him,
The beggar's inn is where the night
o'ertakes him."

Speaking thus, the son, asking his father's benediction, took farewell and departed. At the moment of leaving he
was heard to say :

Wise men who seek a happier life to own
Go to a country where they are not known.

He travelled till he reached the bank
of an impetuous river whose current was
dashing rock against rock, with an uproar heard many farsangs away.

A terrible water it was, so that even
*   the fowl were afraid;*
And a millstone cast in its wave like a
*   feather was lightly conveyed.*

He saw there a group of people, each
one with a little piece of money, squatted
at the crossing, and goods for the tran-
sit packed up. As to our young man, the
hand of giving was closed for him, and
he put forth instead the tongue of flat-
tery, but notwithstanding all entreaty
they showed small friendliness, saying :

No pay no ferry! you can't force us row
Unguerdoned! Give the fare, and fair
*   you go!*

So spake the unfeeling *mallaj*, and
turned away with laughter, continuing :

A strapping swain! But swim the river
*   then,*
Bring one man's money if you talk as ten.

Exasperated at their taunts, the young man desired to be revenged. The boat had put off, but he shouted out that if they would be content he would give them the garment upon his back. The boatman, yielding to avarice, brought the boat back again to shore :

Greed will sew up eyelids of watchful-
ness,
Greed brings the fish and bird into dis-
tress.

As soon as the young man got his hands within touch of the boatman's beard and neck, he drew him close, and without ado knocked him flat. A comrade, who came out of the boat to help, was handled with such severity as to give it up. The boatmen concluded that it would be well to come to terms, and as to the fare, it was forgiven :

When thou seest quarrels, hold afar !
Fair words can shut the gates of war;
Match hasty blood with Mercy's milk,
A sharp sword cannot cut soft silk.

EXCELLENCY OF MODERATION

By gentle speech, and soft, persuasive ways,
Led with one hair, the elephant obeys.

In excuse for the past they touched the hem of his gown, and bestowed false kisses of friendship on his head and face, and, leading him into the boat, put off anew. Presently they arrived at a stone pier in the middle of the water, built by men of Yunân, when the boatmen cried out : "There is peril to the boat! Whoever is bravest and most manly must spring to this stone-work and hold her warp so that we may make a landing." The young man, proud of the courage which he imagined himself to have shown, and forgetting the offended feelings of the crew, disregarded that maxim of the sages : "In whomsoever thou hast caused animosity to arise, albeit it be followed by a hundred acts of kindness on thy part, free not thyself from anxiety of revenge from that single deed—seeing that though the arrow hath been extracted the pain still rankles in the wound."

Quoth Yaktash unto Khîltash—and wiser
words were none—
"If thou but scratch thine enemy, fear
him till life be done!"
When by thy deed another's heart hath
wrong,
Trust not thyself to be at ease for long;
And if against a fort thou fling'st a
stone
Wonder not if another thence be thrown!

As soon as the young man had coiled
the rope round his wrist and leaped upon
the masonry a boatman dragged it from
his hand, and the boat was pushed away.
Helpless and bewildered he remained on
the pillar, and for two days suffered
much hardship and misery. On the
third day a deadly sleep seized him by
the collar, and he fell into the water.
Not until after another night did he
reach the shore, only a spark of life remaining. Subsisting on leaves of trees
and wild roots, he by-and-by gathered a
little strength, and then took his course
into the waste, until, thirsting, hungered,

and feeble, he arrived at a well, where many people were assembled, buying drinks of water with money. Not possessing any, the hapless youth begged hard for a draught, and when it was refused put forth the hand of violence, but in vain. Some of them he struck to the earth, but the others soon overcame him and mercilessly beat and wounded him.

Gnats, in a cloud, the elephant will pierce,
For all he is so sovran and so fierce ;
And ants the lion's skin will eat away,
If Fortune sendeth such a lordly prey.

Broken and bleeding, he fell in with the rear of a caravan, to which, in his necessity, he attached himself. In the evening they came to a spot dangerous on account of robbers. He observed the people of the Kafilat trembling with fear, and their thoughts all full of impending destruction. "Be not apprehensive," he said ; "I am one who can answer for fifty freebooters, if your young men will stand by me." Reanimated by his valiant words, the caravan

people took heart again, and were glad
to be in such company, giving him at
the same time victuals and drink. But
the fire of hunger in the young man's
belly was so fierce, that he ate and
drank hard until the devil of famine
lay quiet inside him, and then slumber
overcame his eyes. An old man in the
company, much experienced, and one
who had seen the world, remarked : "Oh,
friends! I am more suspicious of this
guardian of ours than of the robbers!
Is it not recorded how a certain Arab,
who had amassed a few direms, dared
not to sleep in his house alone for fear
of the Lurian brigands, but brought
one of his neighbors indoors, out of his
dread of solitude? This man tarried with
him for several nights, until coming to
learn where the direms were hidden, he
laid hands on them and went off. In the
morning they found the Arab stripped
of his property and bitterly complain-
ing. 'What can be amiss with thee?'
they asked, 'except that thieves have
carried away that silver of thine?'

'Nay, by Allah!' cried the Arab, 'but it is my friend has carried it away.'

None sits at ease and trusts a snake,
knowing the snake will sting;
But to be bit by tooth of friend, that is
a sharper thing!

"How wot ye, my friends! that this young man is not of the number of the robbers, and hath not, by cunning, got into our midst in order that, at the moment of opportunity, he may carry information to his associates? The better thing, methinks, to do is to leave him here asleep and quickly to depart." This counsel of the much-travelled graybeard seemed judicious to the younger men, being already suspicious of the stranger, and consequently, packing up their goods, they left him slumbering and started off. When the rising sun beat upon his back, he sate up, and perceived that the caravan had disappeared. Much did he wander about without finding a road. Once more parched with thirst and foodless, he lay with his face in the dust and his heart set deathward, mournfully saying :

*They pity wayfarers the least
Who have not been themselves distressed.*

While uttering this, a padishah-zâdah, a king's son, who had been hunting game and had become separated from his camp, came thither, and standing near, heard what the young man said, and seeing his outward aspect good, though his condition was of distress, asked of him : "Whence art thou, and how camest thou hither ?"

The young man related a little of that which had passed over his head ; and the prince made compassionate bestowal on him of a Khilât and some money, and bade a person of trust conduct him to his own place. His father, at sight of him, was overjoyed, and gave God thanks for his safe return. That evening, what had befallen him—the boat, and the violence of the boatmen, and of the villagers, and the deceitfulness of the caravan people—he told it all to his father. "Oh, my son!" said the old man; "spake I not unto thee, at hour of departure, that the strong hand, being empty, is useless, and the lion's strength (without money) is feebleness?"

Well, said the warrior, in his evil hour,
One jow of gold's worth fifty maund of
*   power!*

The son gave answer: "Yet, oh my father! until one confronts difficulty one shall not obtain wealth, and without putting life in peril none can gain victory; and if you never sow grain, you will never fill a granary! See you not that for those small hardships which I endured I have brought back much riches of experience, and for the stings that I bore a plentiful stock of honey?"

Albeit 'tis only once a day we eat,
Needs must we rustle for our daily meat!
The diver, did he dread the sharp-toothed
*   shark,*
Would seldom fetch the white pearls from
*   the dark.*

The lower millstone never moves, and so
Bears its great burden of enduring woe.
What eats a hungry lion in his home?
What quarry to a lighted hawk will
    come?
If in our houses for our bread we wait,
To grow as lean as spiders is our fate.

Quoth the parent: "Ah, my son! on this occasion Heaven hath helped thee, and good fortune hath guided, so that thou hast plucked thy rose out from the thorns, and the thorns from forth thy foot. Moreover, a man of good heart appeared, and showed compassion on thee, and did relieve thine afflicted state. But this is rare, and wonders like it are not to be awaited."

The hunter doth not always kill his prey,
One day the tiger doth the hunter slay.

It is very much as chanced with a certain Sultan of Persia, who had a precious jewel set in an amulet, and being on a jaunt of pleasure with some of his favorites to Masla Shiráz, would needs have them fix the amulet on the dome of Asad, announcing that whosoever with his arrow should shoot clean through it might possess the jewel. It happened that there were four hundred bowmen in the Sultan's surrounding, who all of them shot, and missed. But a lad on the roof of an inn, firing away at random, for sport, sent one shaft which, borne by the breeze of morning, was carried directly through the ring, and to him the jewel was given, with many other marks of favor. The boy, after this, burned his bow and quiver, and when they asked him why, replied, "In order that the glory of my first attempt may continue!"

The counsels of the wise may go awry,
The fool may hit his mark at the first
try.

XXIX

I saw a Darweesh living in a cave, who had shut himself off from the world, no more regarding princes and great men with an eye of fear, nor abating his own dignity for them.

He that sits at door of asking, will be
poor until he die.
He who asks not reigns a Sultan, want-
ing naught, his neck is high.

One of the Sultans of that region had it conveyed to the Darweesh that, believing in the good disposition of holy people, he desired that the recluse would condescend to eat bread and salt at the palace. The Shaikh acquiesced, because to comply with such invitations is conformable with the Sunnat. Afterwards, when the Sultan, on the excuse of some service, visited him, the devotee rose up and cordially saluted his Majesty, embracing him with kindliness. The Sultan gone, one of the Shaikh's companions inquired whether such politeness towards him was not a violation of his rule, and where was the reasonableness of this? The Shaikh replied: "Have ye not heard how they have said:

EXCELLENCY OF MODERATION

If at a good man's table thou shalt sit,
'Tis just to rise and greet the lord of
*   it.*

The ear may go through life and never
*   hear*
One note of drum, or flute, or dulcimer;
The eye may lack the garden's grace,
*   and be*
Unblessed by rose, or vine, or rosemary;
The head which hath no pillow of soft
*   stuff*
May on a stone find rest and peace
*   enough;*
And if no pleasant bedfellow ye own,
Thrust hand in bosom and sleep well
*   alone;*
But bellies are impatient, and rebel
In discontent, unless ye fill them well."

THE GULISTAN

OR

ROSE-GARDEN

OF

SHAIKH SA'DI

𝕲ateway the 𝕱ourth

THE BENEFITS OF TACITURNITY

THE BENEFITS OF TACITURNITY

I

Unto one among my friends I said :
"The resolve hath come upon me to restrain myself in speaking, for the reason
that over and over again one happens to
speak ill as much as well, and the obser-
vation of enemies lighteth only on that
which is ill." He replied : "Ah, brother !
the best of all enemies is he who observes
not the good !"

Virtue in eyes of hatred hateful shows,
And Sa'di seems a thorn instead of rose.
The orb of day, the splendor of the sun,
To the blind bat sheds little light, or
　　none.

O　　　　　　　209

A BAZAAR dealer, having incurred a loss of one thousand dinars, enjoined upon his son not to mention the subject to anybody. He answered : "Oh, my father ! it is thy firmân, and assuredly I will not speak; but acquaint me with the advantage and reason of keeping it secret." Quoth the sire : " In order that our disaster may not become twofold instead of single only, first by losing the money, and next by incurring the remarks of our neighbors."

Tell not your trouble to the enemy !
They chuckle, while " God be your help !"
they cry.

III

THERE was a young man of good parts who had gained good taste of sciences and erudition, and yet withal a modesty so remarkable that he would sit in an assembly of learned people and never speak one word. His father put it to him once : "Why, O my son ! utterest thou, too, not something about the things which thou dost know ?" " I dread," answered he, " lest they should question me, perchance, upon something of which I am ignorant, and that so I might endure reproach."

Hast thou not heard of the Súfi was
*   driving nails in his shoe,*
When a Sarhang seized his sleeve, and
*   cried : "It is you, friend ! you !*
Must rise and be farrier for us !" Be
*   silent, and none will know ;*
But with word and with deed comes need
*   the proofs of thyself to show.*

IV

ONE of high reputation among the most learned, engaged in discussion with an unorthodox person, and, not succeeding against him in argument, flung down the target of fight, and retired. Some one said : " Thou who hast

so much erudition, such skill, such virtue, and such wisdom, how camest thou
to be worsted in contest with this un-
believer?" Quoth the learned doctor :
"What knowledge I have is knowledge
of the Koran, and of the Hadîsh, and
the sayings of the Shaiks ; while he, as
regardeth these, hath neither belief in
them nor patience to hear them ; therefore what profiteth it to me to listen
longer to his Kafir talk?"

Whoso the Koran will not heed, nor the
*   traditions take,*
Best is he answered in disputes when an-
*   swer none ye make!*

V

THALÎNOOS (Galen), observing a rude
fellow lay hold of a wise man's neck and
put him to affiont, said : "If this rever-
end person had been truly wise, things
would not have come to such a pass between him and such an ignoramus."

BENEFITS OF TACITURNITY

*Where both are wise, strife doth not su-
    pervene,*
*Nor will one wise man with a churl be
    seen*
Contending.   If a fool in folly speaks
*The wise by mildness to convince him
    seeks ;*
If both be wise, a hair's enough to bind
*The contact of their wits — in the same
    kind*
If one hath wisdom; but two brutish fools
*Will break an iron chain as well as
    rules.*

VI

OF Subhan Wahil they have spoken
as being in eloquence incomparable.   If
he discoursed for a whole year before
the face of an assembly he would never
commit the fault of using the same
word twice over ; but should a similar
meaning be required, he employed a different expression ; and this is among the
number of the accomplishments of the
companions of princes.

Though a discourse be heart - subduing
  sweet,
Fit to be heard, and for approval
  meet,
Being spoken, let it rest! Too much is
  twice
For sweetmeats and for speech, if once
  suffice.

VII

I OVERHEARD a sage fellow remark :
"None doth his own character of fool-
ishness so plainly declare as the man
who beginneth his own part of the con-
versation before another hath brought
what he had to say to a conclusion."

Discourse, good friend, a head hath, and
  a tail—
Jumble not words with words till noise
  prevail!
A lord of understanding, judgment,
  grace,
Speaks not, till silence make for him a
  place.

VIII

CERTAIN among the attendants of Sultan Mahmud inquired of Hasan Maimandi what his Majesty had said to him that day concerning some business. "How !" quoth he, "do ye not already know ?" "Nay, but," spake they, "thou art minister of the state, and what the Sultan sayeth to thee he doth not deem proper to tell to the like of us." "Quite so," replied Hasan ; "and seeing that my lord imparteth such things, believing that I will not declare a word of it to any one, why did you ask me?"

*Not all he knoweth will the wise man
   say ;
He stakes his neck who with the King
   doth play.*

IX

IN the matter of bargaining about a house, I was wavering, when a Jew said to me: "I am an old house - master in

this quarter; as to the character of
this abode, inquire about it from me, and
buy it on my word, for it hath no fault!"
I answered, angrily, "Except, indeed,
that thou art neighbor to it!"

*Ten dinars of base coin might buy the
  house that's next door to a wretch,
Though to-morrow—if chance make him
  die—a thousand good dinars 'twould
  fetch.*

X

ONE that was poet and musician be-
took him to the chief of a gang of robbers, and recited the praise of that personage. He, in return, commanded the
singer to be stripped of his clothes, and
driven forth from the village. The dogs
also attacked him from behind, and
wishing to take up stones against them
from the ground he found them frozen
hard. Thus rendered helpless, he exclaimed: "What *haramzadah!* What
base-born scoundrels are these, who let

their curs loose, but tie up their pebbles!"
The robber-chief overheard this from a
window, and, laughing merrily, said:
" Ai, man of much sense! Ask some
favor from me!" Says the poet: "I ask
for my clothes only, if thou hast the
bounty to bestow those!"

Get what thou may'st, and be glad, from
them not wont to be givers;
'Scape with thy skin, if thou canst, when
thou dost parley with rogues.

The Sâlar of the robbers became well
disposed towards him at this; restored
to him his plundered garments, and bestowed on him a pûshteen of fur, and
some direms.

XI

A Munjjâmi—a soothsayer—entering
unexpectedly into his house, found a
strange man there, sitting with his wife,
whereat he did mightily abuse the man,
and spake wild words, by which ensued

clamor and calamity. A person of sense, becoming acquainted with the circumstances, observed :

What could he know of sky and stars,
or heaven's all-hidden life,
Who did not see in his own house the
knave that kissed his wife?

XII

A KHATIBIH, a public reader, who had a disagreeable voice, yet fancied it mellifluous, was droning as usual, to no purpose. You would have taken his harsh accents for a croaking crow of the wilderness. The people of the place, by reason of the office which he held, put up with him, not considering it proper to complain, till such time as another of the public readers, who bore him a hidden grudge, came visiting him, and said : " I have had a dream about thee ! May it turn out well !" " What didst thou see ?" asked the man. " I dreamed,"

quoth the other, "that thou didst possess
a pleasant voice, and that at its sound the
listeners had tranquillity." After musing
a little the hoarse-throated preacher observed: "It is a dream of blessing to me
which thou hast beheld, because it hath
made known to me my defect, in that I
have an unpleasant organ and that con-
gregations are troubled when I read. I
make vow that from this time forth I will
read only in a gentle and governed tone."

Ill fall the friends who let my failings go
For merits, silent of those faults they
*   know ;*
Who suffer me to think my thorns are
*   roses,*
And breath such as the jasmine bud dis-
*   closes ;*
Give me instead that sharp-eyed enemy
Who sees me as I am, and makes me
*   see !*

XIII

THERE was one also in the Mosque
of Sanjarieh who made gratis the call

to Namâz, but with an accent that offended all his hearers. The master of the mosque, a just and kindly Amîr, desiring not to grieve him, said : "My good young man! This Musjid possesseth several old Muwazzans, who each receive five dinars a month, so I will give thee ten dinars to go somewhere else." To this he assented, and went away. After an interval he reappeared before the mosque master, and said: "Ay, Khudâwand! Thou didst me mischief sending me hence with these ten dinars, for in the place whither I repaired they do now desire that I shall take twenty dinars and go away from them, but I have not consented." The mosque master laughed, and responded : "Hark ye! Do not accept it, for they will be, by-and-by, willing to offer you fifty."

None with a mattock, shall so scrape a stone,
As thou our spirits with thy raucous tone.

XIV

ANOTHER unpleasantly voiced person was reciting the Koran aloud, when a lord of hearts passed by and inquired of him : "How much is thy monthly allowance ?" "Heech ! Nothing !" quoth he. Said the holy man : "Why, then, dost thou take all this zahmat on thyself ?" "I read," he replied, "for the love of God !" Rejoined the other : "For the love of God read no more !"

If with a croak so damned thou read'st the Book,
The splendor from our Islam will be took.

THE END

www.ingramcontent.com/pod-product-compliance
Lightning Source LLC
Chambersburg PA
CBHW020114030726
47498CB00006B/2102